HALF WOLF

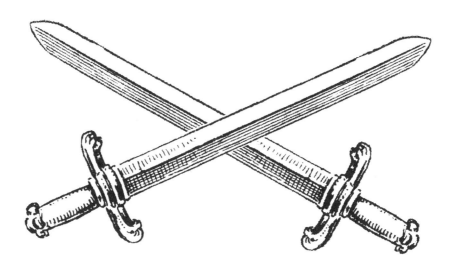

AIMEE EASTERLING

WETKNEE BOOKS

ISBN: 1530440491

ISBN-13: 978-1530440498

CHAPTER 1

Three shifters walked into a bar.

It sounds like the beginning of a corny joke, doesn't it?

But here's a little more information for you. I was those shifters' alpha and den mother rolled into one. Two of the barhoppers were jail bait or close to it. And the establishment in question was filled to the brim with horny, lawless, outpack males.

No wonder I wasn't laughing and *was* in a big hurry.

I breezed past the bouncer with a show of entirely human teeth, then rolled my eyes at his laxness. The employee wasn't being remiss by not checking my ID. Not in a werewolf bar. But he still wasn't really doing his job.

I was twenty-one—barely—which is all humans would have cared about when allowing entrance to a drinking establishment. But the guy at the door in a shifter bar was supposed to turn away anyone without the ability

1

to don fur and howl at the moon. And even though I was technically a shifter, my half-human heritage meant my wolf was too weak to rise up behind my eyes and prove her worth to the bouncer.

Good thing I was accustomed to faking it.

But I wasn't home free just yet. I'd barely set foot in the sea of writhing bodies when one of those lawless males alluded to earlier grabbed my arm, swinging me around to collide hard with his chest. My chin thudded against bare flesh only slightly less hairy than it would have been in lupine form and my nose took in the over-ripe scent of unwashed man.

Ugh. Not that it would have mattered if he was cute. I was on a mission and Ginger, Cinnamon, and Lia had a half-hour head start on me. I could only imagine what kind of mischief the trouble twins and their tagalong cousin could get up to during thirty long minutes alone.

"Nice to see another lady in the place," the male offered with a triumphant leer, clearly pleased with himself for having snagged one of the few females in evidence. His words made it sound like he was trying to pick me up, but his iron grip on my bicep presented a very different picture. Ten feet in the door, I was already in trouble.

Luckily, I was up to the challenge.

"Not interested," I replied sweetly, grinding the heel of one boot into the top of my assailant's arch. I hadn't dressed to impress and didn't particularly expect my hiking shoes to make much of an impression. But I was pleasantly surprised. This particular male must have shown up at the back door in wolf form because his feet were bare. And they were also apparently quite sensitive to being stomped on.

Unfortunately, the shifter didn't so much release me as fling me across the room to land against the legs of another group of outpack males. This time I was the one initiating the collision, and the male I struck wasn't impressed. Snarling, he kicked me out of his path. But at least he didn't look down.

I guess my weak wolf has a few things going for her, I thought as I struggled to my feet. There had to be at least a hundred males in the room and most of them were almost certainly outpack werewolves with no clan—or woman—of their own. A lone female like me in a bar like this was akin to lighting a match beside a powder keg then standing there tapping my foot while wondering if anything would blow.

Luckily, my half-blood skin didn't exude the same sort of come-hither charm as a pure-bred pack princess would have. And, in the dimness of the dance floor, my tomboy apparel probably made me look like just another shifter kid out on his own and hunting for a good time.

Or perhaps the males' lack of attention to my skinny form was the result of vastly more enticing eye candy on the other side of the room. Because I soon caught sight of my three pack mates by dint of following everyone's gazes to a table off to the side of the bar. There, Ginger was belting out an accompaniment to the piped-in music and providing enticing visual aids to prove that tequila did indeed make her clothes fall off.

"Take it all off!" one of the shifters beside me hollered, and the crowd surged forward in one enthusiastic mass. I figured it wouldn't be long before the first horny guy made it past Cinnamon's guard and turned this happy crowd into a bloodbath. So I gave up on pushing between chests and instead dropped down into a crouch, weaving my way around legs as hefty as tree trunks.

Abruptly, I found myself pushed into a corner of the room, my trajectory losing perspective as Ginger's voice was drowned out by roars of encouragement. For a split second, I was back in the tiny cellar where I'd been stuffed by bullying pure-breeds when I was barely old enough to attend kindergarten. *Dark, close, no way out.* Sweat broke out on my forehead and I forced fingers between knees to stop the former from trembling.

Okay, so I'll admit it. My knees were trembling too.

This is absurd. They got themselves into this mess and they can get themselves right back out of it.

My single glimpse of Ginger had proven that her brother was indeed at her back, ready and willing to take on the entire room full of shifters in her defense. The male twin had one hand on Lia's arm too, proving his intent to guard his cousin as well as his sister. Still, the kid had looked scared even as she did her best to mimic Ginger's gyrations.

So, yes, I could pretend that the three teenagers would make it out of there alive without my assistance...even if that pretense would have been a bald-faced lie.

But I just couldn't talk myself into the mental evasion. I'd been abandoned too many times in my life to do the same for members of my own pack.

Plus, I was ostensibly those teenagers' alpha, which meant I was in charge of keeping their flesh attached to their bones. I knew it and they knew it. Why else would Ginger have made the admittedly stupid decision to try out another shifter bar despite the fallout from her last similar attempt? Even she wouldn't have gone off half-cocked if backup wasn't on the way.

So I pulled a deep breath into lungs that already ached from overexertion and I pushed my way back into the crowd.

***

"Ready to go home?" I called up to my pack mates when I finally achieved my destination. Cinnamon was laughing in delight at his sister's antics, Lia had finally discovered the beat, and Ginger had stripped down to a bra and miniskirt with nothing underneath.

I knew the latter fact not only because I could see straight up her skirt but also because she was stepping out of lacy undies and preparing to fling them into the crowd as I spoke. The female trouble twin flicked the aromatic garment away with one finger, and the lucky males close enough to have a chance at claiming the prize fell to the ground in a pile of testosterone-crazed aggression and greed.

Unfortunately, though, most of the shifters wanted a piece of the original, not just a scrap of fabric that had picked up the pack princess's scent. My stomach banged painfully against the edge of the table as I was thrust forward by another surge of the crowd. In response, I grabbed onto the laminated particleboard with grim fingers, doing my best to hold my ground while waiting for my pack mates to come to their senses.

For a moment, Ginger merely smiled at the show. Then her eyes took on a truly wicked gleam as she glanced down at me, proving she wasn't ready to let me off the hook just yet.

"Hey, Fen," she called in greeting. "What a blast, huh?"

Only an hour earlier, I'd begged the nineteen-year-old to pay attention to the way her pack-princess vibe turned our neighbors into animals— sometimes not only metaphorically but also in the flesh. I'd asked that she at least consider her brother's and Lia's safety before jumping into danger with both feet joyfully extended. In response, the trouble twin had rolled her eyes and demanded to know the point of being a member of a free, young pack if I was as much of a pain in the ass as her last alpha.

I'd thought the teenager just needed to gripe and moan, so I'd shrugged off her words. But, no—as soon as my back was turned, Ginger had snuck out to prove her point.

"You win," I yelled up at her now, not sure if she could even hear me over the din of the crowd. "But how do you plan to get Lia out of here alive?"

In response, Cinnamon lowered the sixteen-year-old into my waiting arms, then leapt down off the table to join us. "Ginger's gonna make a diversion so you can break our cuz here free," he yelled into my ear. "We'll meet you around back."

"Not much of an exit strategy," a quiet voice drawled into my other ear. I whipped around to face a tall shifter about my age dressed up in cowboy chic—ten-gallon hat, checkered shirt, huge belt buckle, and nut-hugger jeans. Unlike the hairy-chest guy, this one was cute, but I didn't trust my human intuition to root out his true intentions and my wolf was better off sleeping. Still, Ten-Gallon wasn't grabbing Lia's ass, so I figured he was a cut above the rest of the room's inhabitants.

"Do you have a better idea?" I challenged him.

"I'll boost you out that window," he offered, pointing at a tiny aperture barely large enough for Ginger's hips to wiggle through.

Okay, so the trouble twin's hips matched her boobs—huge and comely. The rest of us would have no problem sliding out.

As long as Ten-Gallon could be trusted at our back, that was. I traded a glance with Cinnamon and my pack mate shrugged in response. Unlike his sister, the male half of the trouble team was laid back to a fault. I could never quite tell if Cinnamon obeyed me because I was his pack leader or just because it was easier to float along on the wave of even my extremely mild version of alpha dominance than to stand against the tide.

So the choice would rest on my shoulders alone, as usual. That was okay—I was used to it.

"Okay, Cinn. You go out first and we'll toss Lia up after you. If anything goes wrong, Glen's got the car idling out front. Get out of here, and Ginger and I will take our chances."

The song was nearing its dramatic conclusion and the crowd was yelling commands at their entertainer so loudly I could barely hear myself think. But when Cinnamon touched his sister's foot and jerked his chin up at the window, I could see the pack princess take in the entire plan in a moment via that ultimate in modern communication—twin speak.

"Okay," she mouthed. Then the buxom shifter produced a diversion as promised. First, she reached forward to fiddle with the front clasp of her bra, releasing her bountiful breasts. Then she spun on high heels to show off the merchandise, a feat that I was pretty sure would have caused me to break my neck even if I wasn't perched atop a table in a crowded bar.

Werewolves are accustomed to casual nudity, but even I had to admit that Ginger's boobs were things of beauty. The outpack males fell silent through pure awe as they took in a show they'd never thought possible—a pack princess emulating a topless dancer. There was no pole to climb, but Ginger did just fine without props, swiveling her hips so enticingly that Cinnamon and Lia made their escape without a single shifter in the room taking notice.

Well, that wasn't quite true. My new buddy and I noticed because we were the ones boosting our companions up toward the unconventional exit. "You next?" asked Ten-Gallon, not quite able to tear his gaze away from the table-top view.

"No, Ginger next." Sure, the teenager seemed quite capable of taking care of herself. But I was her alpha. Which meant that I would also be the last to leave this sinking ship.

Of course, I knew the minute the metaphorical curtain came down, the crowd would turn nasty. But there was no getting around the inevitable. We'd just have to move fast and take our chances.

I sprang up on the table to join Ginger, boosting her toward our new accomplice's waiting hands.

"No way!" "Boo!" "Hey!"

The cacophony of displeasure abruptly ceased as Ginger stepped out of her final item of apparel, allowing the tiny skirt to drift down and settle upon the table. Then she turned to blow a kiss toward her doting audience.

The pack princess was now buck naked and every male in the place—Ten-Gallon included—roared his approval.

Then Ginger was slithering out the window to join the rest of our clan, leaving me as the only pack mate still in danger. Well, me and Mr. Ten-Gallon Hat, who wasn't looking like such a good defense against several dozen hyped up and disappointed outpack males.

This may be the time faking it isn't quite enough, I thought inanely. And then my stalker walked through the door.

CHAPTER 2

His wolf was large, but it wasn't the beast's size that stilled the crowd. Instead, a concerted wave of goosebumps crashing across every shifter in the room proved that the newcomer's alpha dominance was single-handedly responsible for throwing metaphorical cold water over the proceedings.

Of course, alpha dominance was nothing new in the werewolf world—everyone had the ability to some extent. Still, a shifter's capacity to sway others to his will was largely dependent upon the relative strength of each contestant's wolf. My weak animal half, for example, could have been barked down by anyone in the room...which is why she was currently sound asleep within my human body.

At the other extreme, the eddies of invisible yet very tangible compulsions rolling off my stalker's lupine form proved that he was the rarest of the rare—an uber-alpha. The newcomer's dominance was so intense that he was able to part the raucous shifters like the Red Sea with a single glance, leaving a clear path between the door he'd padded through and the table on which I crouched.

In fact, if the evidence around me was any indication, I should've been glad my own wolf was asleep or I'd likely have fallen flat on my face at my stalker's approach. The rest of the room's inhabitants weren't so lucky. Some of the nearby shifters remained rooted to the spot. Others dropped to their knees, heads bowed to the floor. And a drunk in the corner nearly choked on his own vomit until the stalker's gaze followed mine and released the shifter from his spell long enough for the poor guy to finish throwing up.

While the uber-alpha was looking the other way, I glanced up at the window through which half of my pack had recently disappeared. Perhaps this was my chance to escape?

But Ten-Gallon was as frozen as the next guy, and I knew our rescuer would be torn to shreds by his fellows as soon as my stalker left the room. I didn't even know my new comrade's name, but a budding leadership sense suggested that he would soon become our pack's newest member.

Which meant I was going to have to suck it up and deal with the wolf who was responsible for my outpack status and who seemed intent on following me across the country in order to gloat. His eyes latched back onto mine as I pondered my options, and I could tell I wouldn't have made it out the window anyway before his teeth closed around my skin. So, as usual, I settled on bravado as the best solution to a bad situation.

"Hunter," I greeted him.

In response my stalker shifted so fast I couldn't even discern the transition, hair receding and body lengthening in an instant until only his amber eyes remained the same. "Lost Wolf," he countered.

And with those simple words I was flung back three weeks to our first meeting. Then, as now, the uber-alpha had walked into a room vibrating with peril. Then, as now, I'd felt duty bound to protect my pack even while risking my own skin.

But at that point in time, the danger had come from Hunter himself.

Come to think of it, I wasn't so sure anything had changed.

**

When Hunter and I first met, I was a happy-go-lucky member of a different clan entirely. Our alpha was kind but firm, our pack was quite capable of protecting its weaker members from all comers, and my wolf spent nearly all of her time asleep.

Despite that pastoral tranquility, though, half of my days involved patrolling the pack's boundaries to make sure potential dangers didn't encroach. So when I discovered the aforementioned uber-alpha in lupine form nosing through trees half a mile from our village, I immediately bared my human teeth and shouted out a challenge.

"Stop there!" I demanded. Never mind that I couldn't back up my posturing with any alpha dominance of my own. I'd learned that simply lifting my chin in challenge and speaking like I meant it usually did the trick. And, sure enough, the huge wolf slinking through the undergrowth paused and cocked his head in response.

Without the sensory assistance of a rampant inner wolf, I'd just assumed the stranger was an over-zealous drifter trying to decide if our clan was open to new members. We generally were, but we also preferred supplicants to come in through the front door rather than sniffing around behind our backs. So I was terse when I stalked over, grabbing his ruff with one hand and clenching down on the top of his muzzle with the other. "Rude," I growled, shaking the stranger as if he was a puppy and I was his alpha. "Come with me."

Hunter obeyed easily enough, letting me drag his furry butt back to my alpha without complaint. Only when I saw the latter's tense body language did I realize the error of my ways. It seemed I'd misread the stranger's crooked grin as submission and had invited a predator into our den by mistake.

A den into which a young pup soon ambled, throwing us all into a tizzy of over-protectiveness. Any shifter who got my alpha's hackles up was one I didn't want hanging around youngsters. Unfortunately, my weak lupine nature meant that I wasn't able to physically protect the kid in question or to boot the stranger out the door. So I resolved the issue in the only way I knew how—by continuing to pretend like I was far more wolf than I could ever dream of being.

"Family matters," I told the stranger as my pack leader turned his attention to the pup. Grabbing the uber-alpha's newly materialized hand, I pulled him over to a chair in the corner and away from the kid who had caught his eye. Perhaps if I was able to sidetrack our guest for a few minutes, my alpha could shuffle the youngster back out the door and then take this explosive bundle of handsomeness off my hands.

This time around, though, my playacting was a little less confident than usual. After all, if my alpha—who possessed the strongest inner beast I'd ever seen—was concerned about this stranger, then Hunter could likely bark and I'd offer up my finger bones to be used as toothpicks. I shivered, but still put pseudo-command in my voice when I spoke. "Talk to me."

The uber-alpha feigned obedience once more, but I got the distinct impression that he was only humoring a shifter who he found intriguing. "Talk about what?" he asked. His voice was so deep it seemed to rumble through the air and into my belly like heavy bass, and I had to clench my jaw in order to ignore the tantalizing sensation.

"How about your name?"

I was definitely in over my head but the stranger seemed to enjoy my spunk. He took one of my hands between his much larger paws, sending yet another tremor through my body. "I'm Hunter."

"Is that your name or what you do?" I couldn't resist asking. And now Hunter's smile finally reached his eyes. The uber-alpha was obviously impressed by my perspicuity, even though he really shouldn't have been. I had no choice but to be alert to the subtle cues of body language since I couldn't depend on my inner wolf to clue me in. And it wasn't as if the stranger was trying to hide his thoughts either.

"Both," he confirmed. "And you're Lost Wolf."

"No, I'm Fen," I answered, ripping my hand out of the stranger's grasp before my brain caught up with my mouth. I knew I shouldn't be antagonizing a shifter so strong he gave my alpha heart palpitations, but it offended me that Hunter had so easily seen into the core of my being.

Okay, so "offended" probably wasn't the right word. It scared me to death. It made me mad as hell. And, yes, it also pleased me no end that someone had finally seen what none of my pack mates had cared to notice during the last twenty-one years of my existence.

While I was trying to work through all of those contradictory emotions, Hunter elaborated on his analysis. "You're different and lonely. You're looking for a place to fit in."

"Oookay." I did my best to brush off his words even though each one struck like a dart into my soul. "Did I accidentally sign up for a therapy session?"

I feigned checking the planner on my cell phone, but fumbled the device instead since I wasn't able to tear my eyes away from the shifter in front of me long enough to complete the pretense. The phone hit the ground with a clatter that made me jump but didn't seem to affect anyone else in the room.

"You're uncomfortable," the stranger said after a moment of silence. "You don't want to talk to me."

True and true. But the kid who Hunter wasn't supposed to interact with was still in the room and my alpha continued to radiate distress. So I shook my head. "No, I'm *dying* to have a pleasant conversation with you."

And that was, unfortunately, true as well. "But we've just met. Ever hear of small talk?"

"Sounds trivial and inconsequential."

"And you sound like you swallowed a thesaurus."

I couldn't feel the effects, but I'd gotten used to the glassy eyes and clenched jaw that signaled a shifter exerting his or her alpha dominance. So I wasn't surprised to see the kid flinch on the other side of the room as Hunter's gaze bore down on me.

In response, my wolf stirred groggily awake deep within my body. And for the split second that she was less than completely comatose, I was able to fully understand the power of the werewolf before me. My nostrils flooded with the intense aroma of cold, wet sassafras, as if I'd been immersed in a vat of chilled root beer. And I felt an overwhelming urge to lunge forward and kiss the uber-alpha on the lips.

Then I pushed my wolf so hard she was flung backwards into the dark recesses of my mind and washed off her feet by the flood of my subconscious. As her presence faded, so did Hunter's compulsion.

"You know it's sexual assault to force a woman to kiss you against her will, don't you?" I snarled. Then I whispered under my breath: "And pretty darn desperate too."

What I really wanted was to punch the guy, but I had a sinking suspicion he wasn't human enough to respond chivalrously to a blow from a lady. And if Hunter decided to fight back, I'd be dead. So I stuck to the defense that made me feel strongest—verbal sallies.

The uber-alpha cocked his head to one side curiously, then responded. "I only asked you to let your wolf do what she wanted to do," he rumbled, and I flushed beet red. "Surely that's not against two-legger rules?"

Yep, he'd definitely won that round.

But I wasn't ready to roll over and show my belly just yet. When in doubt, ignore the facts and go for the jugular.

"You're a bastard." I ground out the words while leaning subtly forward and shoving myself into his personal space in a shifter provocation. *Take that, you uber-asshole. How often do you get challenged by a wolf you can't smack down with your voodoo powers?*

And Hunter chuckled. In fact, he laughed so long and so hard that tears streamed out of his eyes in rivulets, making his chiseled jawline glisten.

I should have taken the opening I'd been given and run with it. At least the uber-alpha hadn't immediately responded to my not-so-witty comeback, which gave me a momentary advantage.

But, instead, I found myself using every iota of self-control I possessed to refrain from reaching out and drying my companion's cheeks. There was just something about seeing the uber-alpha cry that didn't sit right with me, even if the tears were those of mirth instead of pain. And even if his laughter was, apparently, at my own expense.

But drying his eyes would be nearly as stupid as kissing him, I reminded myself, the latter possibility still niggling at the back of my mind. Actually, swiping my finger across his perfectly proportioned face would be considerably more stupid since I couldn't chalk the action up to his earlier compulsion. *Nope, not gonna go there.*

While I'd been squashing my baser urges, Hunter had been getting a handle on himself as well. And now he was the one to reach out and very gently run one calloused finger across my cheekbone and down the side of my jaw in an unconscious mirroring of the gesture I'd just imagined.

"You...are...intriguing." He paused between each word, so the short sentence lasted until his fingertip drifted across the sensitive skin surrounding my mouth. A fragment of rough callous caught on my softer flesh and pulled my bottom lip very subtly open.

Immediately, my unruly brain offered up the mental image of sucking Hunter's finger into my mouth to taste. Would his skin possess the same root-beer flavor that imbued the air when my wolf was awake and Hunter was within range? Or would he taste even better?

Let's not get carried away, I told myself. *He's an uber-asshole. The pup is in danger. Eyes on the prize.*

So, instead, I snapped my teeth together aggressively, only realizing after the fact that the missed bite could just as easily be construed as flirting rather than giving warning. In response, Hunter cocked his head to one side again before returning hand to lap without continuing the caress.

And I don't regret that. Nope, not one bit.

"You'll never fit in here," my companion said at last, the words grim and spoken as if from hard-won personal experience. "But I know a place where you'll belong."

"This is my pack," I shot back. Now I wasn't just pretending to banter. I was honestly angry that this uber-alpha who knew nothing about our clan would insinuate that my friends treated me differently just because I was a half-werewolf instead of a pure-breed.

Okay, sure, so my ex had recently dumped me for that very reason. But it wasn't as if I'd find a better situation out in the cold, hard world. Former boyfriend aside, most of my current pack mates were willing to embrace my differences and accept me for who I was. That level of tolerance wasn't the case in 99% of the shifter clans out there.

"You're willing to throw away the possibility of true acceptance due to fear of the unknown."

It wasn't a question, but I answered it anyway. "I'm not *afraid.*" I bared my teeth as if my wolf was rampant behind my eyes and was itching to tear out my opponent's throat.

Which wasn't so far wrong, except that my human self was the aggressive one. The uber-alpha didn't need to know that my wolf was currently and would in the future continue to be nearly always asleep.

Hunter just smiled, this time with his lips alone. "The offer's open."

And then the wolf pup we'd been protecting scurried out of the room, allowing me to hand that combination of eye candy and impending train wreck back over to my alpha to deal with. Hunter was far too enticing for his own good, and I was glad to see the back of him even though he seemed to have my best interests at heart.

"Seemed" being the relevant word. Because less than twenty-four hours later, the uber-alpha returned to our territory just in time to cast me out of the only pack where I'd ever felt safe. It turned out that the bastard was not only powerful, he was also an enforcer for the regional governing body known as the Tribunal. In other words, Hunter harnessed enough clout to keep even my scary-strong pack leader in line.

Unfortunately, my entire clan and I had all been knowingly breaking the rules for the past few months. We'd chosen the morally correct decision over the legally correct one, keeping that little pup safe rather than returning her to a sadistic father who—by shifter law—owned the kid as thoroughly as he owned his fancy new car.

The Tribunal was responsible for resolving inter-pack altercations, so they'd sent Hunter out to pass judgment on our sinful ways. And rather than exploring all the shades of gray in the situation, the uber-alpha had decided to stick to the letter of the law. Which meant we got to keep the pup...but either my pack leader or his mate would be put to death to even the score.

So I'd stuck my nose in where it didn't belong and had caught the backlash in their place. The upshot? My alpha would continue to run his pack as a haven for oddball werewolves like myself...but I would no longer be included in the family photos. Instead, I was set adrift to wander through outpack territory with only my weak inner wolf to protect me.

Or so Hunter had mandated. But my previous pack leader had one last trick up his sleeve. Ripping away part of his own alpha dominance, the shifter who I'd always looked up to presented me with that shred of power plus four underlings to back up my claim to pack-leader status. The thin veneer of danger settling around my shoulders might possibly be enough to keep lawless shifters from chewing me up and spitting me out...or at least from swallowing me whole.

Unfortunately, we all knew my chances of survival as a halfie female in outpack territory still weren't worth betting on. The presence of companions just meant I'd be dragging more innocents down with me when I inevitably crashed and burned.

And the whole mess was Hunter's fault. He'd acted so cordial and interested in me when we'd first met. Then, even after ostracizing me from my former home, he'd continued to reel me in. Taking my face between his huge hands, he'd promised: "You'll thank me later."

Even then I thought he'd kiss me.

But he didn't, the bastard. Just left me yearning and lonely on the edge of what he clearly thought was a brave new world and what I knew was a death sentence for myself and for my new pack.

I hadn't seen him since.

CHAPTER 3

Not so fond memories aside, I opened my mouth there in the bar to remind Hunter that my name was Fen. F-E-N. Surely three little letters weren't too much for his wolfish brain to handle?

But before any snark could emerge, an overwhelming scent of rotten bananas filled the crowded room and five of the frozen shifters around us abruptly transformed into wolves with an audible pop. Then the outpack males' growls merged into one ominous rumble as they stalked forward, progress only slightly hindered by the sea of torpid bodies between them and their prey.

Oh, and in case I wasn't entirely clear—*I* was their prey.

"I think that's our cue to leave." Hunter must have sprinted to reach me so quickly. But when I looked down from my table-top perch, the enforcer didn't appear out of breath. Still, his usual lackadaisical attitude had worn thin, suggesting that the uber-alpha was as shaken as I was to see his compulsion overthrown. Given the fact that Hunter was the strongest werewolf I'd ever met, he'd probably never lost a battle of wills before.

As a consolation prize, I accepted the uber-alpha's hand even though I didn't need any help descending from the table. A zing of awareness rushed up my arm at the contact and our eyes locked for a split second. Despite the unexpected attraction, though, I planted my feet when Hunter began tugging me toward the door.

"We're not leaving without Ten-Gallon."

"Ten-Gallon?" my stalker queried. One thick eyebrow rose quizzically and I gestured with my chin toward the man who'd helped Ginger, Cinnamon, and Lia escape.

Hunter considered the buff shifter for several long seconds, then shook his head decidedly. "No, I don't like the look of him. And you don't even know his name. Hurry up."

The uber-alpha's words were a terse command and I had to literally bite my tongue to prevent myself from saying *You're not the boss of me* and flipping him the bird. Instead, I turned away and prepared to make my stand, drawing the sword gifted to me by my previous alpha. If Hunter wasn't going to help my new pack mate survive the ensuing altercation, then I would.

The ring of steel emerging from its scabbard halted the enemy wolves' forward momentum momentarily, but now we had an extra half-dozen combatants arrayed against us. All were much closer than I would have liked, too, while Hunter and I still appeared to be at an impasse. Not good.

"Are you going to unfreeze my buddy or run away and leave us here like a scaredy cat?" I demanded without taking my gaze off the approaching danger.

Hunter seemed torn between commenting on my juvenile language and on the three-foot hunk of metal I'd been learning to use in lieu of wolf form. Then he shook his head and sighed out an "okay" that promptly sent

Ten-Gallon sprawling at my feet. Keeping the sharp blade carefully clear, I leaned down and gave the fallen werewolf a hand up.

"Much obliged, ma'am," the cowboy shifter said, doffing his hat. "I'm Quillen Atwater, by the way. But you can call me Quill."

See? Chivalry isn't dead, I wanted to tell Hunter. But the rotten-banana scent was growing stronger by the second, and the sound of enemy werewolves shaking off the uber-alpha's mental grasp now resembled the clatter of corn in an air popper just before the kernels achieved critical mass. So instead, I simply offered my own name back to Quill and led the three of us down the shifter-free aisle between table and door at a speedy walk.

Without further comment, the uber-alpha dropped in behind Ten-Gallon, pacing backwards while warily scanning the crowd we passed. I half expected him to shift into lupine form to expand his arsenal, but instead, Hunter remained human and weaponless, even deigning to offer a conversation starter.

"That reminds me..." the uber-alpha began, and I couldn't quite prevent myself from interrupting. My companion just sounded way too calm and in control in the face of what looked like it would soon become a bloodbath.

"What reminds you? The fact that we're being stalked by twenty angry werewolves?" Because at least that number of shifters had now reanimated. One reached toward me in human form, and I swiped at his bare arm, giving my opponent just enough of a scratch to warn without causing an emergency-room visit. The wounded shifter lifted his human lips into a lupine snarl and I got the unpleasant impression that he was filing my face away in his mental database to make future vengeance easier. *Great.*

"Exactly," Hunter replied easily. "You're not safe here. Someone's been kidnapping ha..." He paused, abruptly realizing he'd almost used a common slur for half-breed werewolves right in front of one. "Um, I mean, human-werewolf hybrids...."

To my discredit, I let the uber-alpha flounder as we continued walking carefully toward the door. It was nice to be able to embrace the upper hand for a few seconds, but I put him out of his misery soon enough. "You can call it like it is. I'm a halfie and proud of it."

"Hmm," Hunter answered. Then he regained his composure and continued. "As I was saying, *halfies* have been going missing around these parts, but more so further east. Some were males, but most were young, attractive females like you. You're headed in the wrong direction. You need to take your pack and go back the way you came."

Now it was my turn to growl. I hated nothing more than being told what to do, even though the "attractive" part sounded nice. "I'll take it under advisement," I said between clenched teeth.

Then time for conversation abruptly ran out as the first wave of advancing shifters reached the aisle and began trotting toward us at a steady clip. I eyed the door—close, but not close enough. We wouldn't all be able to sprint to safety, but maybe at least one of us could.

Grabbing Quill's arm, I pointed him in the right direction. "*Run!*" I ordered, putting my own mild alpha compulsion behind the command. My genetics meant I shouldn't have been able to command so much as a field mouse, but my previous alpha's gifted mantle did the job...this time at least. I sighed in relief when the cowboy shifter turned to obey, then listened until the clatter of his shod feet was abruptly muffled by the safety of grass and dirt.

Almost there. Four pack mates had now made it out of the bar alive, so I only had myself and Hunter to worry about. Luckily, I was pretty confident the two of us could take care of ourselves.

I expected the uber-alpha to think differently since he apparently considered me to be a damsel in distress. Instead, he surprised me by pushing my body between himself and the advancing wolves. "Hold them off for a minute and I'll see if I can reactivate that freeze," he ordered.

I was torn between being thrilled that the uber-alpha trusted me enough to depend on my protection and being annoyed that he didn't seem to know how to pose a request in the form of a question.

No, wait, I was none of the above. Instead, as thirty—yes, the number had grown yet again—slobbering werewolves advanced upon me and my thin blade of metal, I knew exactly how I felt.

Terrified.

***

I was well aware that my previous pack leader, Wolfie, had handed me his grandfather's sword as a metaphorical symbol of my newfound power. But I'd focused on the more practical utility of the weapon right away.

It wasn't so surprising that Wolfie and I didn't see eye to eye on the purpose of my new katana since we were about as different as two werewolves could be. My old alpha was a bloodling—a shifter born in lupine form who tended to retain those wolfish characteristics for the rest of his life. His alpha dominance alone could always bend troublesome shifters to his will, but he never hesitated to don fur if he needed sharp teeth in order to prove a point.

So Wolfie probably had no clue how defenseless my submissive wolf made me. And how unsuited I was to running a pack.

Unfortunately, I couldn't just yank out the fur and claws when threatened like everyone else could. Sure, I was *capable* of transforming into a four-legger. And even though my animal half was more likely to turn tail and run than to fight, I could overcome her urges with my human brain and get the job done. The sublimation caused a subtle slowing of our reaction time that had negative consequences at critical moments, but it was better than nothing.

Still, I almost never shifted because my wolf was just too darn weak to be shown off in public. Specifically, I couldn't risk her being barked into line by more dominant shifters...and, newly gifted mantle aside, every single shifter's animal half was more dominant than mine. So I didn't have the option of taking advantage of a werewolf's typical physical defenses—teeth and claws.

Back in my old clan, the halfie disability hadn't been much of a problem. Wolfie had protected our pack with a gentle yet strong dominance that put the worries of weaker wolves to rest. Even at the worst of times, I'd always known someone was guarding my back.

That all changed when Hunter's manipulations thrust me into the position of watching out for four—now five—other werewolves. And I still couldn't use lupine teeth to get my way.

So as soon as Wolfie presented me with his family heirloom, I got to work. I streamed YouTube videos on my phone and practiced while my new pack slept until I fell to the ground exhausted time and again. Only Ginger had noticed the strange nicks on my legs, but she appeared to accept the explanation that I'd cut myself while shaving. And eventually I became skilled enough that even those signs of fumbling disappeared.

Which is all a long way of saying—I *did* know how to handle the sword I was carefully grasping between two sweaty palms. But it felt very different to hack at a tree trunk compared to swinging at living, breathing shifters, even if the latter seemed ready to tear out my throat.

Here's hoping I can just wave the scary sword menacingly and buy Hunter time to do his work, I thought without much faith in the possibility. Sparing a glance over one shoulder, I saw that the shifter in question had stretched out flat on the ground and appeared to be meditating...or perhaps taking a nap. Not a good sign.

"She looks tasty." I couldn't tell which of the shifters had spoken, but a rumble of agreement rose from both men and wolves alike. So I guess the identity of the speaker didn't really matter after all.

"A little skinny for my tastes." This time I caught the eye of the man in question. Speaker two was in his thirties and brimming with good health. In fact, I would have thought he was cute if he wasn't obviously undressing me with his eyes and finding me wanting. *Ew.*

"But serviceable," the first voice countered. "You heard the man—she's a halfie."

A word that had seemed almost charming when emerging from Hunter's lips now cut me like the blade of Wolfie's sword. But I couldn't let them know their barb had hit home. Instead, I lengthened my spine and swung at an encroaching four-legger, this time failing to soften the blow at the last moment.

A whoosh of displaced air, half of a furry ear flying across the floor, and a yelp from my opponent proved that those weeks of practice had paid off. The injured wolf jerked backward like a stepped-on puppy dog before remembering his audience. Then he growled, reversing his retreat even as blood began streaming down the side of his face.

"That was a warning blow." I was proud to hear that my voice was calm and steady even though the more powerful werewolves in the audience would be able to hear my heart beating a mile a minute. "This sword is sharp and I know how to use it. I recommend you all back away while you have the chance."

Voice number one laughed. "Spunky, aren't you?" The shifter in question emerged from the crowd at last, and it was instantly clear that this was the other mens' leader. "That'll make you even more fun when we have you on the altar."

I shivered as my gaze flicked over my opponent's form. Even without the help of my wolf, I could see the wildness of a rampant lupine half within the enemy's eyes. And his stance was relaxed as he strolled casually within range of my sword as if the weapon didn't even exist.

I should've taken the chance and cut him down then and there. Sure, the shifter looked like any other aging businessman. Dark suit, expensive haircut, fancy shoes. But I could feel the evil emanating from his cold, hard eyes and my gut told me the world would be a better place without this particular shifter in it.

Unfortunately, I couldn't quite make myself take advantage of the opening presented. Yes, I'd killed a man before and with this very sword to boot. Still, my previous opponent had been menacing a toddler and, by extension, had been a danger to our entire pack.

And despite that clear-cut motive, I still had nightmares about the sickening crunch of blade through bone, the sucking sound as flesh parted and blood gushed.

They say your first kill is the hardest. But I had to disagree. It's the second, when you knew what to expect, that makes even a brave wolf hesitate.

And, as I mentioned before, my wolf was anything but brave. So I wavered.

In response, the man smiled...then knocked the sword right out of my hands.

CHAPTER 4

"*Freeze.*"

The shifters, the air, and even the beer in nearby bottles responded to Hunter's command. I could feel my teeth chattering despite my comatose wolf. And when the uber-alpha grabbed my hand and yanked me toward the exit this time around, I paused only long enough to scoop up my sword before obediently stumbling along in his wake.

The outside world embraced us in a cloud of humid warmth and I gasped in a long breath, only then realizing that I'd forgotten to breathe for the last several seconds. Or perhaps my autonomous nervous system had also responded to the uber-alpha's command. Whatever. It just felt good to be alive.

My relief was short-lived. "Unhand her," came Ginger's familiar voice, laden with an equally familiar snarky overtone.

I straightened, taking in the scene before me. My entire pack now stood between us and our idling station wagon, three angry shifters plus Lia and Quill off to one side looking a bit befuddled. My comrades had clearly been ready to storm in and rescue me from the barflies, so it hadn't taken much effort to transfer their aggressions to the uber-alpha who still clutched my hand in his over-sized mitt.

I considered pulling my fingers free, knowing the gesture would soothe my pack's ire. But I couldn't quite talk myself into severing our contact. There was just something about Hunter's solid warmth that made me feel better after that heart-stopping display inside.

Plus, I wasn't quite sure I could move yet. *Good excuse.*

"I think you have the wrong idea," the uber-alpha said quietly. He might have squeezed my fingers very subtly at the same time, as if he didn't want to relinquish our bond quite yet either. But his attention remained riveted on my pack and a low growl underlay his words. Hunter didn't like to be challenged.

After scanning all five faces, the uber-alpha apparently decided that Ginger was the one in charge. His gaze locked ominously with the trouble twin's...which is when I noticed that she was still entirely naked. Even clad, the teenager's perfect curves had been known to turn males of both shifter and human persuasion to stone, so I thoroughly expected my companion's eyes to wander south rather than maintaining their challenge. But, instead, Hunter's attention remained resolutely focused above the teenager's neck.

Maybe he checked out the merchandise while I was gasping for air? It was the only reasonable explanation.

And, more relevantly, if my brain was up to snarky mental comebacks, chances were pretty good I could talk again. So, with a shiver of regret, I released Hunter's hand and herded everyone else toward our waiting vehicle.

"I don't know how long the freeze will last," I said, "so we need to make tracks. Ginger can drive. Quill, you'll come with us?"

The cowboy shifter tipped his hat at me in cordial assent. But despite his good manners, this still wasn't quite the way I'd planned on picking up new pack mates.

We couldn't really afford to trust the newcomer sight unseen, so I shot a questioning glance at Glen and was relieved when my most solid pack member nodded back. My second then proceeded to subtly rearrange seating order so Cinnamon took the middle back seat, separating Quill from our weakest member—the twins' younger cousin. At least that thorny issue had been easily taken care of.

I kept one eye on the closed bar door, wishing we could just jump in the car and make tracks. But a speedy escape was impossible when our vehicle was already stuffed to the gills with all of the pack's worldly possessions. Some decisions would have to be made if we wanted to clear space for extra bodies.

Still, after three weeks of living in each others' pockets, we worked together like a well-oiled team. So it took mere minutes to clear a space in the far-back for an extra shifter to perch. Out went the cooler containing tomorrow's breakfast and lunch. Out went the huge tarp we needed to keep our tent dry when camping in a soggy spot.

Out went a tremendous duffel bag full of Ginger's clothes. You'd think as skimpy as her preferred garments were, they wouldn't take up much space. But the trouble twin's tank tops and short shorts made up in quantity what they lacked in bulk.

"Hey!" the clothes horse protested, and I shot her the stink eye in return.

"You and your wardrobe fill a similar square footage," I answered. "It's up to you who stays behind—you or your clothes."

Our banter was normal, but the worried glance I shot toward the bar door was not. Which was probably why Ginger gave in so easily. "Whatever," she grumbled, averting her gaze. But she still obeyed my veiled command, pulling the bag open and picking through in search of something to put on in case we ran across human cops who would be confused by a naked driver.

Although, actually, that might be a good way to avoid the ticket we invariably ended up with when Ginger was behind the wheel.

Second-to-last problem solved, I turned back around to face Hunter at last. He was still two-legged, but his face was averted from my little pack as if he were preparing to shift back to lupine form and flee the scene as soon as the car left the lot.

Taking a deep breath, I touched the uber-alpha's bare arm to capture his attention. "How about you?"

Truth be told, I was even more torn about inviting this abnormally strong werewolf along for our grand escape than I had been about including the cowboy shifter in our little band. Because Quill was a known entity—an outpack male likely looking for a mate and a bit of power. Trouble, but in a manageable (and cute) package.

Hunter, on the other hand was a conundrum, but one whose motivations were beginning to show through the murk. After all, how could he have shown up right in the nick of time to save our hides after weeks of separation if he hadn't been following us around in the first place? That suggested a level of dedication to the project that I suspected vastly exceeded the stick-to-it-iveness of the average outpack male.

And then there was the issue of the tremors my handsome stalker regularly sent down my usually shiver-free spine. The intense physical reaction to Hunter's presence didn't bode well for my own future sanity.

Still, the uber-alpha would be in as much danger as anyone else once the outpack males woke up, and I had a feeling that even his intense alpha dominance wouldn't hold the angry werewolves off for long. My stalker had almost certainly arrived on foot, and I doubted he could outrun his opponents indefinitely. So there was really only one ethical decision here.

"Hunter?" I prompted.

"Do you want me to come with you?" he countered.

The uber-alpha was the furthest thing from weak, but something about his words brought to mind the insecurity that had underlain my former pack leader's first interactions with his mate-to-be. Hunter was a bloodling as well, I now realized, and as a result he probably wasn't the most adept at human social behavior. Perhaps some of his semi-psychopathic mannerisms stemmed from simple discomfort while wearing a two-legger's skin.

You're reaching, I admonished myself. But, still, I nodded even as I heard the first angry shouts emerging from inside the bar.

"Yes, I want you to come along."

***

Ginger drove like a mad woman. We screeched around curves, blew through red lights, and once we were on the interstate our intrepid driver did an admirable job of pissing off truckers by cutting in front of them and then slamming on her brakes. Amid all the mayhem, the trouble twin slowly but surely shook every last barfly off our tail.

And, then, once the final outpack male was a distant memory, the real trouble began.

"So, what are your intentions toward Fen?"

Glen's throaty murmur from the far-back area of the car barely carried to my shotgun position, and Ginger cleared her throat irritably. Her lupine-assisted ears wouldn't have had any trouble picking up the conversation, but she knew as well as Glen did that my own hearing wasn't similarly enhanced.

Agreeably, the latter raised his voice when he continued. "Well?"

Widely spaced streetlights above the highway cast alternating bands of light and dark, and I took advantage of one of the latter to swivel in my seat and glance across the car's inhabitants without being too obvious about it. Lia was sound asleep with her head on Cinnamon's shoulder, and her pillow looked only vaguely more aware of his surroundings. But Quill nodded a greeting from directly behind my seat. And the two shifters in the far-back were erect and alert, bristling with barely contained antagonism.

"My intentions?" Hunter's voice was quietly sarcastic, as if Glen was an overzealous waiter who had dared to ask for his movie-star customer's autograph. "I'm not sure I understand your question."

"Oh, I believe you do," Glen countered. "We've smelled you around our campsites from the beginning. You never come close enough to invade a traveling territory...not quite. But you're always there. Watching. Waiting."

This was news to me, and I shot a glance at Ginger. A well-placed streetlight illuminated the trouble twin's unsurprised face, proving that she had also known about our stalker's presence.

The teenager shrugged apologetically as she met my eyes. "Didn't seem relevant," she answered my unspoken question.

It didn't seem relevant that the uber-alpha who had pushed us so abruptly out of Wolfie's safe clan and into outpack territory had been dogging our heels for the last few weeks? No, what Ginger and Glen really meant was that there was no point in worrying their so-called pack leader since my mild alpha dominance couldn't do anything about the potential danger. Hunter's menacing uber-alpha skills were entirely out of my league.

But now wasn't the time to delve into *that* issue. Not when our car contained two strange werewolves who might or might not have ulterior motives for befriending us. Hunter and Quill didn't need to know about the rot at the core of our little pack.

Instead, I held my breath and waited to hear how Hunter would respond to Glen's demand. It didn't take long, and the uber-alpha's words carried so admirably that it was clear he was aware of his larger audience. "And why do you care?" the uber-alpha demanded, his words projecting an almost tangible bite. "Are you her father? Her brother? Her *mate?*"

In response, Ginger's hands twitched on the steering wheel and suddenly our tires were vibrating across the rumble strip and out of the right-hand lane of the highway. I lunged for the plastic-coated wheel across the trouble twin's suddenly frozen form and righted our progress.

"Hunter!" I demanded through clenched teeth.

"Oops." The word was so quiet I almost thought I'd imagined it, but then Ginger's hands abruptly tightened beneath mine, proving that the uber-alpha had relinquished his control over the car's inhabitants. Meanwhile, a gasp from the far-back suggested that Glen had regained the ability to breathe as well.

Any sane shifter would have backed down in the face of Hunter's extreme alpha dominance and obvious lack of human control. But Glen instead answered firmly, if a bit breathlessly. "I'm Fen's *pack mate*. I deserve to know."

"Pack mate." Hunter rolled the word around in his mouth, tasting it as if he'd never considered the notion before. "Is that why you followed a weak halfie woman into outpack territory? Not because you're looking forward to wresting away her position and becoming an alpha in your own right? Not because you want to claim three beautiful women as your own?"

Glen's strangled growl was the uber-alpha's only reply, and I thought for a moment that we were going to have to stop the car so I could place my body between the two males in an effort to prevent bloodshed.

But, instead, I saw Hunter pat the other shifter on the shoulder in an almost-apologetic expression of cordiality. "No, I guess not," my stalker continued. "Well, then I'll answer your question since you're Fen's *pack* mate." The subtle emphasis on the word "pack" wasn't lost on any of us.

Then Hunter's warm, deep voice embraced me out of the darkness. "I never have seen the point of a pack," he mused, his voice becoming quieter but not so much so that I couldn't catch every word. "But," he finished, "Fen *is* my mate."

CHAPTER 5

Ginger growled loudly enough for Hunter to hear her at the other end of the car, and then my inner wolf awoke with a vengeance. Usually, I had no trouble squashing my lax lupine half, but I was so exhausted from the preceding drama—and from the fact that it was close to three in the morning—that my control over the animal must have slipped.

She, on the other hand, seemed to be rejuvenated after swimming through the murky sea of my subconscious mind for the past few hours. Plus, the wolf was apparently a big fan of the uber-alpha in the car's far-back. I barely prevented her from pushing fur out of our skin then leaping over the intervening seats to reach him. And when I pushed my animal half back down inside me, I was pretty sure she didn't entirely fall back asleep this time around. *Time to get off the road.*

"Take this exit," I ground out between clenched teeth just as the skies erupted into a sudden downpour. I'd been planning to push on for at least another hour, but traffic signs were barely visible now between frantic windshield-wiper strokes, so it looked like now was the time to stop after all.

I flipped on the dome light for a split second to peer at a shifter-specific paper map—you won't find information like that on google. I was pretty sure we were just barely encroaching on the territory of the mild-mannered Franklin clan, which meant we'd likely be safe for one evening at least. The werewolves in question probably wouldn't even notice our trespass, or if they did would forgive us once Ginger batted her long dark eyelashes and jutted out her well-endowed chest.

We'd cross that bridge when we came to it, though. Because my eyeballs were so scratchy I thought they might start to bleed and I couldn't afford to let my wolf take over while there were two strangers in the car.

Speaking of my lupine half, she'd drifted back up to join me behind our human eyes, and I did my best to nudge her into sedation. But she sidled away from each of my advances, and I honestly didn't have the willpower to chase her down while simultaneously trying to ensure the car didn't end up in the ditch.

So I closed my eyes for a split second to gather my composure then shouted into Ginger's ear to guide her toward the campground I'd circled as a potential stopover point. It was cheap, run-down, and had a terrible rating on trip advisor—just the kind of place for a bedraggled, broke band of werewolves to hole up for the night.

The rain was still pounding down just as hard ten minutes later when the car pulled up to the accommodation's pay station. We rolled to a stop beneath the small canopy and the abrupt cessation of staccato raindrops on the roof woke Lia from her nap. "Are we there yet?" our youngest member asked sleepily, rubbing one brilliantly blue eye with a slender fist.

Instantly, Hunter and Quill's attention latched onto the girl's face as if she'd offered them a five-course dinner. The trouble was that, even though Lia was a halfie, her golden tresses and gentle nature tended to attract male werewolves like flies to honey. This wasn't the first time the rest of us had been forced to step up and defend the girl, but it *was* the first time danger had been pointed in her direction from within our own ranks.

In unison, Ginger, Glen, Cinnamon, and I all growled. In response, Quill looked away with shame on his face. "Sorry," he murmured. The uber-alpha, in contrast, made no move to release Lia from his hungry stare.

"Hunter, Quill, let me introduce you to Lia," I said, just in case our point hadn't yet been suitably elaborated upon. "She's a half-blood like me. And she's *sixteen*. Hands off."

Quill seemed suitably chastened, going so far as to flinch away from the enticing teenager as if he'd been burned. But Hunter only smirked as I challenged him with my gaze. "Perhaps you didn't hear the part about *you* being my mate," the uber-alpha murmured almost too quietly for my human ears to pick up on.

"You may be on a diet but that doesn't mean you can't read the menu, eh?" I countered, rolling my eyes. "Whatever. But, take it from me, Hunter, you have *no reason* to be on a diet." Then, realizing that my words made it sound like I was giving the uber-alpha permission to court Lia after all, I hurried to add: "And Lia's still off limits."

Ginger saved me from sticking the rest of my leg into my mouth when she pulled the lever at her feet to pop the hatchback, releasing Glen from his cramped prison. It couldn't have been pleasant to ride in such a small space shoulder to shoulder with a scary uber-alpha, but my comrade gave no sign of tension as he jogged over to the pay box. "Ten bucks," he called back toward us, "for five humans."

"And two dogs," Ginger agreed, already stripping out of her clothes in preparation for a shift. "Got it."

It was handy to be able to lower our numbers by dint of a quick transformation. But the ten dollars, it turned out, were harder to come by. My wallet was entirely bare since I hadn't budgeted for spending money on two different campsites in one night. Ginger had, predictably, used up every last penny she owned to get her little group into the shifter club. And Glen's pockets were equally empty since he'd been the one to pay for gas most recently. There was no point on cadging off Hunter since the uber-alpha had shown up in lupine form and couldn't even claim the clothes on his back, and I didn't really feel comfortable asking non-pack members for funds anyway.

"Leave a note that we'll pay with a credit card in the morning," I said at last, defeated by the knowledge that I'd once again been forced to utilize Wolfie's get-out-of-jail free card. It wasn't that my previous alpha couldn't afford to fund our subsistence-level existence, nor would he gripe over the expenditures of cash. But it just wasn't done to have one clan's essentials paid for by another clan's alpha. Instead, the credit-card usage was one more sign of my total ineptitude as a pack leader. It chaffed like a wet pair of skinny jeans.

"I've got it," Quill said quietly before Glen could obey my command. The cowboy shifter's large hand briefly touched my shoulder before he pulled out a leather wallet that appeared to be bulging with cash. For a split second, I thought my lupine-assisted nostrils caught a hint of rotten bananas, but then I realized it was just my over-tired brain playing tricks on me.

"Thanks." I hadn't meant my gratitude to sound so grudging, but it was hard to put myself into yet another outpack male's debt. Still, we needed to set up camp and bed down if we planned to hit the road again bright and early the next morning. It wouldn't do to trespass on the Franklins' good nature any longer than was absolutely necessary.

So I forced the monetary issue out of my mind and let my gaze scan the rest of the crew. "Who else wants to be a pet dog tonight?"

"We've already got that covered," Lia answered quickly. Her words were muffled since she'd turned away from me to pet the huge gray wolf that nearly filled the far-back area of the car and I almost leapt across the seats to still her hand. Knowing I couldn't get there in time, though, I instead opened my mouth to warn the kid off. You *don't* pet werewolves, and nothing about the uber-alpha's body language suggested he was willing to take the dog pretense beyond the bare minimum.

But Lia tended to get away with murder in a very different fashion than Ginger did. The latter batted her eyelashes and froze the male brain quite effectively. In contrast, nobody wanted to bark the trouble twins' timid teenage cousin down, least of all me. It was too much like kicking an already whimpering puppy.

And, apparently, Hunter felt the same way. Because he accepted Lia's caress and didn't even glance up when Ginger's furry body jumped up onto the carpeted floor beside him.

"Where to now?" Glen asked as he slid into the driver's seat to replace the trouble twin.

"There's a site around back that's almost hidden in the woods," I answered, checking my cell phone one more time to make sure I'd chosen the optimal location. "The bathroom is a long way off, so I doubt any humans would have parked there. Take the first right-hand turn, then drive to the very end."

***

It was pitch black as we set up camp, and the rain still hadn't let up. Regardless, the original members of my pack weren't slowed down by excess water. Lia and I unpacked the contents of the top carrier, spreading bundles and bags out across the empty seats of the car so our belongings didn't become saturated with rainwater as we handed off each item in the proper order to Glen and Ginger. They in turn fed items to Cinnamon, our tent-savant, who soon had a canvas abode erected in a spot that was as dry as our current storm allowed. At that point, everyone began lugging mats and sleeping bags into our temporary den, relieved that another long day was nearly at a close.

As for the outpack males, Quill tried to help but mostly got in the way while Hunter disappeared into the damp darkness as soon as the car rolled to a stop. I wasn't entirely surprised in either case. It would take a while for Quill to learn the ways of our group and Hunter probably didn't even see the point of trying to blend in.

The question was—did either male *want* to join us permanently? In most cases, it would go without saying that a male drifter would be thrilled to hook up with a pack that was sixty percent female. But a halfie alpha and the lack of a defined territory made our clan less than enticing. Plus, I wasn't entirely sure whether we wanted to expand our numbers in the first place, so the question might have been moot.

"I appreciated the ride."

The words came out of nowhere, and I jumped, hitting my head on the roof of the car and making my inner wolf whimper. Lia had joined the hauling crew, leaving me entirely alone in the dark confines of the pack vehicle. And when I whirled around, I found myself mere inches away from a dark shape that blocked off the open door and my path to freedom.

For a split second, I was terrified. Then I noticed the broad hat shielding the cowboy shifter from the weather. It was only Quill.

I sighed in what should have been relief but what was actually disappointment. I'd seen neither hide nor hair of Hunter in twenty long minutes, and it would have been nice if I could have believed that the uber-alpha was the male currently seeking me out for a one-on-one conversation.

In your dreams.

My wolf wanted to pursue that line of thinking, suggesting that she really *had* been dreaming about the scarily strong shifter. But I shushed her at the same time I reassured the man who was standing in front of us in the flesh.

"No problem," I told Quill. "We appreciated your help in the bar." I paused, then decided to get the issue over with. "Were you wanting to travel along with us for a while?"

"If you'll have me." The cowboy shifter's words were a soft drawl that charmed me as much as his willingness to pay for our campsite had hit the spot half an hour earlier. Still, adding a new pack member wasn't a choice I planned to make on my own.

I opened my mouth to tell him so when a flashlight flickered to life a hundred yards away through the trees. Someone was walking around the bend our car had taken not long ago, and my weak wolf offered no clues as to whether that someone was human or shifter.

It could easily be the first wave of barflies come to tear us apart, or a Franklin outguard demanding our immediate decampment. Or perhaps the light represented a new danger I was too exhausted to dream up at the present moment.

Speaking of new dangers, a growl emerged from the darkness directly behind me. I tensed, then realized this third intruder was only Hunter lurking in the shadows in lupine form. He padded over to stand beside the car door even as Quill clued me in about the other newcomer's identity.

"Human," he offered. "Smells like an older female, smoker, overweight."

Probably the campsite host. "Go tell the others," I ordered, wanting at least one unknown out of my hair while I dealt with another. I eyed Hunter, considering sending him away as well. But the inevitable power struggle seemed like too much effort, so I instead unfolded myself from the back seat and stood with the uber-alpha by my side as the older woman paced toward us through the rain.

"Terrible weather," she called as she came within human hearing range. The umbrella over her head sported cartoon suns and storm clouds barely visible through the real rain, making a mockery of her words. Then, as she stepped a little closer and her flashlight played over Hunter's and my wet forms, the human emitted a little "Oh!" of surprise.

I'd like to think the older woman was turned off by my companion's massive lupine form, but I had a feeling she was instead responding to the tattoos lining my forearms, to the gashes in the thighs of my jeans, and to my unruly hair. Looking tough was helpful for a weak halfie trying to hold her own amid werewolves, but the persona wasn't so handy when dealing with the general public.

So I emulated Quill and layered on the charm in order to mitigate my unfortunate first impression. "I'm so sorry we woke you up, ma'am. We'll be unpacked in a couple more minutes and then you won't hear another peep out of us." As if she possibly could have noticed our quiet voices above the pounding rain, but apologies often set humans at ease.

Predictably, the campsite host's tense shoulders visibly melted. "Now that's okay, dear," she said, and for a moment I thought she might pat my hand. But then she caught another glimpse of my ink and thought better of the gesture.

Or maybe she was responding to the way Hunter stepped subtly between us so she'd have to reach over his sodden head to get to me. *Bad doggy*, I thought but was a bit too chicken to actually say the words aloud.

"Um, well," the woman backpedaled, "I was just checking to make sure there's nothing you need. Oh, and here." She held out a soggy paper sack, and even my human nose could catch the distinct scent of warm chocolate-chip cookies inside.

Hungry, my wolf whispered, and I only realized we'd reached out to grab the food too quickly when the campsite host jerked her arm away as if she'd been stung. Dratted wolf.

Still, the woman recovered quickly in the face of my copious thanks. "Some *trolls* have been leaving bad reviews of our campground online," she continued, wrapping her mouth around the word "troll" with an effort as if she was repeating a phrase recently introduced into her lexicon by a hip grandchild. "There's a flier in the bag with a list of common review sites," she added. "If you enjoy your stay, I hope you'll consider logging on and putting in your two cents' worth."

The request seemed so ludicrous. Here we were fleeing from dozens of angry werewolves, shaken up by the idea that a serial killer might be targeting halfies, and trying to decide whether Hunter and Quill were more likely to protect our backs or eat us while we slept. Meanwhile, my own wolf was as out of control as a mild-mannered beast like her could be. Plus, who knew whether Hunter was one of those alphas who used the term "meat" about humans, killing them for sport or simply to relieve boredom.

And in this mess of danger and confusion, our campsite host was concerned because her business probably averaged a three-star review rating?

Still, the cookies smelled good, if damp. So I shot the older woman an honest smile. "I'll be sure to do that," I offered. And I didn't even wait until she'd turned her back before I dug into the bag of warm treats.

CHAPTER 6

I opened my eyes the next morning to a horrendous sight. A young woman, naked, chest ripped open and blood splattered in every direction. She appeared to have been caught midshift, with lupine ears starting to burst out of a human head and with her hands already replaced by paws. There was no question that the victim had once been a vibrant shifter with a long life ahead of her. And now she was dead.

It isn't real, I told my queasy stomach, pushing the cell phone and the appalling image it contained away from me. "What the heck?" I demanded aloud.

I was too upset to soften my voice, and all around me both furry and furless heads popped up out of our heap of werewolf slumber. The grisly wakeup call had my heart beating way too fast, so I allowed myself a second to calm down by making sure everyone was present and accounted for. Yep,

Lia and Cinnamon and Glen and Ginger were all within arm's reach, enclosed by the tent's curved walls. And as long as Hunter and Quill hadn't stolen our old clunker while we slept, then our pack could chalk up one more successful survival of a night in outpack territory.

"What's with the horror show?" I asked more quietly now that I'd gotten my breathing back under control. My eyes locked with Ginger's, unsurprised that the female trouble twin had been the one to stuff her cell phone in front of my nose at dawn. (*Dawn!* Didn't she realize we'd probably only fallen into bed three hours earlier?) In response, the teenager reclaimed the device, flicking through a few screens before showing me what might have been the same girl...had all of her body parts been intact.

"Couldn't sleep." The trouble twin shrugged as if it went without saying that if she suffered from insomnia then the whole pack should as well. "So I decided to poke around online and see if Hunter was telling us the truth. And he was. This girl, Daisy, went missing from the Rambler pack two weeks ago. She showed back up yesterday morning with her heart ripped out of her chest. They think it was *eaten*."

Beside me, Glen growled and I patted his furry head in consolation before jerking with my chin to suggest he shift. My usual backup was solid in human form, but his wolf sometimes had a tendency to overdo the chivalry. Today, I definitely needed him calm and in control...and that meant I needed him two-legged.

Once Glen's body began to morph away from fur, I returned my attention to Ginger and asked the question I didn't really want to hear the answer to, at least not right at that moment. Lia was looking on with wide eyes, which made for an unfortunate audience to such a grim conversation. But the girl was a halfie just like I was, and if she was going to wander through outpack territory then she needed to know what kind of dangers she faced. "Any others?" I asked quietly.

"At least half a dozen," the trouble twin replied grimly. "There's..."

"More like twenty."

The growling voice came from outside our canvas walls and I was glad Glen had shifted seconds earlier or my right-hand man might have ripped through the fabric to fight off the intruder. We really couldn't afford another tent, though, and I instantly understood that the voice didn't represent any immediate threat. So I grabbed Glen's wrist to hold him back and merely muttered "Once a stalker, always a stalker" under my breath.

My words eased the tension around me as my pack mates came to the same realization I'd achieved seconds earlier—that Hunter was the one hovering outside our den's walls. Not that the uber-alpha should be easily dismissed, but at least he wasn't actively working against us.

Or so I thought. Ginger apparently disagreed.

"You seem to know an awful lot about this serial killer," she said grimly, raising her voice to make sure the words carried beyond the tent walls. "Care to elaborate?"

"To tell you about Daisy Rambler, eighteen-year-old half-blood who was so badly terrorized by her pack that she built a little hut half a mile away in the woods?" Hunter's voice was cold now and I pulled the sleeping bag up to my shoulders in hopes the fabric would warm my soul. "To tell you that her family didn't even realize she'd gone missing until she'd been absent for an entire week, that even then they thought she'd run away and hesitated to contact the Tribunal. That I found her by following the scent of carrion through the forest. And when I returned the rotting corpse to her clan's loving arms her alpha didn't even bother to build the girl a funeral bonfire. Is *that* what you want to know?"

The uber-alpha seemed personally affronted by the halfie's mistreatment both before and after death and I had a hard time accepting Ginger's insinuation that he might have somehow been involved in Daisy's dismemberment. Still, it was hard to forget that Hunter had seemed equally caring and interested at our initial meeting and yet he'd still forced me out of my clan and into outpack territory the very next day. As an enforcer whose authority was backed up by our regional governing body, Hunter's word was law both inside and outside of our pack, and he could have easily let us wiggle out from under the requisite punishment for our law-breaking three weeks earlier. So I had to admit I didn't really understand his motivations at all. Maybe Ginger was right and our tagalong companion actually *was* conning our entire pack.

The inhabitants of the tent fell silent for a moment as we took in the uber-alpha's words. Then, at last, Hunter spoke again. "Someone is killing halfies to steal their power, and you're the strongest halfie around. Now can you see why I want you to go west, not east?" He paused as if trying to decide how to turn a command into a question, finally settling on: "Will you, Fen?"

My name on his lips did the job my sleeping bag hadn't, providing the strength to straighten my spine and remember that I had a pack to protect. For a moment, warmth seeped through uncovered limbs as if the uber-alpha's eyes were roaming across my body...which was a ludicrous fancy since Hunter was outside the tent and the early morning light was so dim he probably couldn't tell which shape was me in the first place. Still, the uncomfortable feeling put a bite into my words as I got down to the business I'd already been planning to deal with as soon as my friends awoke.

"That's none of your affair since you're not a member of this pack," I countered more harshly than I'd originally meant to. "At least not yet," I added, mitigating my tone slightly. "Maybe you could give us some space so we can decide whether we want you following us around?"

Hunter huffed out a snort that said as clearly as words: *And how would you stop me going wherever I want to go?* But I heard no other sounds pushing into our temporary domicile. No receding footsteps. No slam of the car door as he crawled back into his own bed.

"Hunter?" I asked after a moment's pause.

"I'll wait," he rumbled. And this time Glen wasn't the only one to growl. Ginger had her hand on the zipper of the tent and looked intent upon heading out naked to whoop the uber-alpha's ass, in fact, before I shook my head at the girl to bring her back into line.

The trouble twin flicked her long maroon tresses back over one shoulder in annoyance, but she conceded the point. Still, when she settled back down, the young woman made a point to slide closer to Lia as if she planned to protect her cousin with her life. "Let's get on with it," the redhead grumbled. "Can we vote Hunter out first?"

"No, Quill first," I responded, ignoring the twin's incendiary language. Truth be told, I hadn't quite decided what I wanted to do about my own personal stalker, so the cowboy shifter seemed like an easier choice to start off with. "The question is, stay or go. Glen?"

My second-in-command shrugged. "Probationarily only, right?" he asked me. And, when I nodded, he mirrored my movement. "Okay, then. We could use more muscle around here. And we can always let Ginger beat him up if he sets his feet the wrong way."

Glen had a good point. Our pack was light on wolf-power, with only him and the aforementioned Ginger really up to the task of protecting us from trouble in lupine form. Cinnamon was always willing to defend his sister's back, but he was a lover not a fighter and tended to pull his punches. And Lia and I were, unfortunately, worse than useless in that department due to our half-blood heritage.

"Cinnamon?" I asked next, moving my gaze around the tent. The male trouble twin met my eyes for only a split second before turning to his sister and raising his eyebrows in question.

"Sure, I like him," Ginger said, her voice purposefully loud as if she was speaking to Hunter rather than me. And her twin followed her lead, although without the attitude, voting in the affirmative as well.

We'd already reached the majority quorum required to allow Quill a spot in our clan, so the issue was pretty much settled. Sure, I had the right to overrule the others since I was technically the leader of our little pack.

But, honestly, I liked the cowboy shifter too. He was polite, soft-spoken, and had paid for our campsite. He'd fit right in.

So I was shocked when I turned to Lia and found the girl shaking her head vehemently back and forth. Then, in the tiniest voice imaginable, she cast her vote. "No," the girl whispered. "I don't want Quill to come with us."

***

"What did he do to you?" Cinnamon demanded, scaring Lia even more by grabbing her shoulder and spinning her around to face him. I expected Glen to counter this display with his usual voice of reason, but my most steadfast companion instead lunged forward as if he planned to latch onto the girl's other arm and replicate the trouble twin's assertive behavior.

Before the kid could get ripped in half—and before the swearing outside the tent grew any louder—I slapped the guys down with my mild alpha dominance. "*Stop it.*" The words wouldn't hold them in place like Hunter's would have, but at least the bee-sting-level compulsion should snap my pack mates out of their posturing.

Sure enough, Cinnamon and Glen both inhaled deeply, the former unhanding the kid and the latter merely pulling her in for a brief hug before letting her go as well. Hunter was still muttering under his breath outside, a dull rumble that circled the tent to stop mere inches away from our pack's youngest member. But the uber-alpha seemed content to let me speak, so I ignored him and crouched down so my face was level with Lia's. "*Did anything happen?*"

The kid shook her head slowly and it took a moment for her to gather her thoughts. "No, I just don't like the way he *looks* at me." I could barely hear the words with my human ears, but I had a feeling Hunter had picked them up just fine by the way his swearing changed over to a deep growl. Our uninvited guest must have turned wolf in his agitation.

"Did Quill say anything?" I asked now. "Try to get you to go off alone with him? Touch you where he shouldn't have?"

"He shouldn't touch her *anywhere*." Hunter's angry words proved he was human again. I was starting to lose track of his lightning-fast transformations, something an ordinary werewolf could do perhaps once in an hour if he was strong and well-trained. But nobody had ever said Hunter was an ordinary werewolf.

"Ignore the peanut gallery," I said, filing the uber-alpha's frequent shifts away to be analyzed at a later date. "*Did* Quill touch you, Lia?"

The kid kept her eyes trained on the ground and merely shook her head. No, it appeared her disapproval of the cowboy shifter was a gut reaction only. And while I didn't like to ignore her intuition, everyone else seemed okay with adding Quill to the pack. Which suggested Lia was just young, inexperienced, and overreacting.

Yes, I'd seen Quill's covetous gaze last night. But the cowboy shifter had also seemed to accept my admonishment and I'd noticed him keeping a greater distance from Lia afterwards. The unfortunate truth was that the girl was going to get those hungry looks from pretty much any outpack male. And given the fact that females were probably few and far between in his life, it was hard to hold the cowboy shifter's initial reaction against him.

So I made the decision for all of us. "Ginger will train some manners into him," I promised our youngest member. "And like Glen said, we're only letting him in on probation. So if anything happens, Lia—anything at all —you can tell us and we'll kick him out. Okay?"

"Okay," the girl whispered, and I hoped I wasn't making the wrong decision.

Still, the clock was ticking. Every minute we spent in the comfort of our tent debating our next move was another minute that the barflies could use to track us down. We needed to get back on the road ASAP, and that meant deciding which, if either, of the two strange males was going to ride along with us as we traveled to our next destination.

"So, Quill's in, tentatively," I continued. "How about Hunter? You can vote with thumbs up or thumbs down since he's sitting *right outside the tent* and listening to every word we say." I raised my voice in annoyance, but the uber-alpha only laughed. And my pack mates, as usual, ignored the nuances of my request.

"I like Hunter," Lia said, her voice a little louder than it had been previously. "I want him to come with us."

I rolled my eyes. The timid halfie was terrified of the charmer Quill but was thrilled to have an uber-alpha in the pack? I'd never understand the minds of children.

"Ginger?"

"Definitely out," the red-head responded, her eyes sparkling with passion. "We don't need him and we don't want him."

"What she said," her brother quickly chimed in.

My gaze turned to Glen at last and he tilted his head to one side in consideration. I could see my beta doing the same math I'd engaged in a few moments earlier. If he voted pro-Hunter, then the tie-breaking choice would be up to me. And I somehow didn't want to be the one to say that the uber-alpha had to go.

And yet...the uber-alpha had to go. He was too strong for our young pack to handle and we had too little understanding of his purpose in following us around to trust him at our backs. In short, Hunter was a danger to our clan, so we couldn't welcome him into the fold.

Nodding his understanding of my dilemma, Glen sealed Hunter's fate. "Tentatively, probationarily...I say no. Hunter is out."

CHAPTER 7

I expected the uber-alpha to be annoyed. What I didn't expect was the flood of invective that came surging out of his mouth, some of the words so intensely imaginative that Cinnamon felt moved to cover up Lia's sensitive ears. Ginger, on the other hand, was clearly taking mental notes, and I had to admit the female trouble twin had a point. Hunter's language was almost poetic in its pure, unadulterated filth.

"Dude, tone it down," Glen growled. "We don't want the campsite host to come back over here and check on us." *Not while you're standing outside our tent buck naked*, he didn't have to add. We all knew that our attempt at appearing human was in serious jeopardy if the uber-alpha didn't get himself under control. So this time around, I didn't naysay my pack mate as Ginger pushed open the tent fly and stepped out into the morning air.

Then the trouble twin began to swear as well, which is when I fumbled for the sheathed sword I'd stuck down inside my sleeping bag and hightailed it out the door as well. The sight that met my eyes pulled a few choice words from my lips to join the invective soup before I started barking orders.

"Cinnamon, Ginger, you're together. Glen and I will team up with Lia. Do what you have to do, but I want one of these invaders captured alive. We have to figure out what's going on." Finally, as an afterthought: "And please try not to wake up the cookie lady."

At last, I returned the entirety of my attention to the outpack werewolves who were stalking out of the mist in lupine form. There were at least half a dozen large, menacing animals present, and the faint banana aroma that drifted off their bodies suggested some or all of the invaders had been present in the bar that Ginger led us to the night before. Our enemies had been beaten once and now didn't seem inclined to hash out our differences with words. Instead, the shifters arrayed against us were out for blood.

Clothes flew off in record time, and soon I was flanked by five friendly werewolves, evening the odds somewhat. "Where's Quill?" I asked, and in response Hunter jerked his chin toward the bathhouse barely visible between the trees. The uber-alpha didn't bother to shift and elaborate, but I guessed the cowboy shifter had gone to take a shower while the rest of us were voting on his future.

Here's hoping our newest member won't be blindsided by a battlefield when he comes strolling back into camp, I thought. But I couldn't really find it in myself to regret Quill's absence. When it came right down to it, pack size wasn't everything. Instead, if given the choice, I'd always go for fewer werewolves who I could really trust at my back rather than for larger numbers of loose cannons.

At the thought, my hand drifted down to settle upon Hunter's head, although whether I was considering him a trusted companion or a loose cannon was up for debate. Immediately, the huge wolf craned his neck to gaze back up in my direction before returning his attention to the outpack shifters who were drawing ever closer to our small clan.

Despite my reservations, I had to admit that our newest companion's presence made me feel stronger. Sure, Hunter epitomized unpredictability. But he also might turn out to be our secret weapon. Soon, the attackers would be close enough to be growled into submission without waking the campground host...assuming the uber-alpha felt like saving all of our skins rather than just his own, that was.

At the thought, I couldn't prevent my fingers from tightening around one fuzzy ear in a silent plea for help. I didn't really expect Hunter to understand what I was asking, nor did I expect him to obey even if he did understand. But, to my surprise, the uber-alpha accepted my subtle direction with alacrity.

I could almost hear the human words in his lupine bark as the booming sound rolled out across the campsite in near-visible waves. And the command *should* have frozen every enemy in his tracks. Even though the uber-alpha's attention had been pointed in the opposite direction, in fact, Cinnamon and Lia cringed away from the noise, their feet growing a little unsteady beneath them.

But the outpack males just kept advancing, parting the fog with their bodies as they drew ever closer on silent feet. Now I could see that each boasted a collar around his neck, a characteristic that struck me as distinctly odd under the circumstances. Equally odd, but more understandable, were the splashes of neon color nearly hidden by the folds of each lupine ear.

"They're wearing ear plugs," I said softly for Hunter's benefit. That explained why the uber-alpha hadn't been able to use his strong compulsion auditorily—the other shifters had arrived prepared for such an attack. But perhaps our not-so-secret weapon could still stare down each enemy individually if he could force the wolves to meet his eyes.

Hunter glanced up at me, and it was almost as if he read my mind. Nodding once, the uber-alpha set off toward the lead shifter, dancing around the latter as the enemy strove to keep his head averted. And rather than helping their compatriot, the other wolves parted to surge around the strange battle of wills and continue with their own advance.

Hunter's ploy would likely work, I suspected, but it would take time to hit all six enemy werewolves one by one. The rest of us needed to pull our weight and defend ourselves in the meantime. So I unsheathed my sword and jerked my head to motion Cinnamon and Ginger away from the tent. In response, the duo slunk off to the side in preparation for flanking our attackers while Glen and Lia drew in closer to me.

Then the campsite descended into such savagery that I could no longer keep track of what each member of my pack was doing. There were wolves everywhere, the enemies' strange silence making their curled lips and sharp teeth appear even more ominous. Two sprang toward Lia from either side in a pincer maneuver and Glen and I worked as a team to drive them back, he with his fangs and I with my sword.

After what felt like hours but was probably less than five minutes, pain threw me off my stride as one of the enemy shifters latched onto my leg, breaking through my jeans to pierce the skin below. I raised my sword, unsure where to cut in order to harm but not kill the beast. But before I could decide, Lia had slammed into the enemy's shoulder and knocked him aside while Glen took the beast the rest of the way to the ground.

In the ensuing lull, my slender young savior looked up at me with such question in her young eyes that I couldn't quite make myself take her to task for diving into the skirmish. It went against all my instincts to allow a sixteen-year-old to fight for her life. But Lia's wolf wasn't quite as submissive as my own, and she'd just proven herself to be both able and willing to defend not only herself but me as well. So who was I to say a halfie had no place in combat?

"Thanks," I said instead of voicing the dueling emotions that swirled through my mind in the battle's split-second pause. And I could have sworn the girl's shoulders broadened ever so slightly at the praise.

Then, to my dismay, she darted away to flank Hunter, who had frozen one wolf and was now playing a game of cat and mouse with another. The halfie watched the action for several long seconds, then repeated her previous bulldozer maneuver, this time throwing the enemy onto his side just long enough to prevent him from evading the uber-alpha's medusa-like gaze.

Two wolves down, six to go. Because my leg-biter had evaded Glen's grip, and I saw now that my initial head count had been off as well. A quick survey of the campsite turned up eight enemy shifters, which meant their lessened numbers still matched our own.

And the enemy was already regrouping. Our remaining attackers split into two parties, one zeroing in on Lia and the other on me. They'd unerringly set their sights on the two halfies within our clan, which probably meant there was a dominant werewolf present who was able to pick out the specifics of our lupine souls beneath our skins. That same alpha would also be able to bark all of us except Hunter into submission, which was a danger to keep in mind since our side hadn't thought to don earplugs.

Can't deal with that now, I reminded myself. *We'll just cross that bridge when we come to it.*

"*Glen, go with Lia,*" I commanded instead of worrying about the issue. I didn't want the girl to be left dangling in the wind during her first altercation, especially not when she appeared to be a person of interest to our enemy.

Sure, Lia was fighting alongside Hunter. But the uber-alpha didn't seem to understand pack dynamics in the same way the rest of us did. *I never have seen the point of a pack,* he'd said the night before, words that later haunted me as I tried to fall asleep in the dark tent surrounded by my own clan members. If Hunter didn't believe in a pack, what *did* he believe in?

Glen, on the other hand, was ultra-protective of every member of our little clan...me included. He struggled against my compulsion for a moment, clearly unwilling to leave me alone with only a sword to defend against the three strong wolves stalking ever closer. But eventually my second followed my gaze with his own and conceded the point. Just before the enemies blocked the last possible escape route, he sprinted off to the side to join up with our pack's youngest member.

That's the point of a pack, Hunter, I wanted to say. *From each according to his ability. To each according to his need. In other words, we have each other's backs.*

It wasn't an issue the uber-alpha and I could hash out right then, though. Not when three outpack males were currently lunging toward my feet with murder on their minds. I flicked my sword back and forth through the air, cutting a long gash in one wolf's shoulder and nearly skewering another before I pulled the blow. I hadn't forgotten our need to take at least one of these shifters alive for questioning, nor did I want to add another notch on my belt and more nightmares to my already interrupted sleep.

And, apparently, our enemies felt the same way. Because the trio of shifters facing me could have easily surged forward en masse and ripped out my throat. But they seemed willing to play a game of attrition instead, waiting me out until I conceded defeat.

It won't take long, I admitted. Already my arms were growing tired from the weight of my weapon, and the first fumbled thrust would give these wolves the upper hand.

Then Cinnamon and Ginger materialized out of the fog. The trouble twins' lupine fur was tinged with red, the coloration not as strong as their vibrant hair in human form but equally eye-catching. And I couldn't help smiling as I took in their grinning faces. Ginger's teeth were bloody, but she was clearly having a blast. And Cinnamon was always glad to protect his sister's back. As an added bonus, neither looked ready to fall over from exhaustion the way I was either.

As soon as she came within range, in fact, the female wolf bounded up against the hindquarters of the smallest enemy, a younger specimen who was lagging slightly behind his compatriots. Ignoring the other two attackers, the trouble twins continued to focus on the loner, Ginger grabbing him by the ruff and shaking while Cinnamon went in for what could have been a killing blow to his jugular. Instantly, the enemy stilled, rolling over to show his belly in a juvenile show of submission.

He's just a kid, I realized. But I didn't have time to pay closer attention to the twins' efforts because the battle raging right in front of my eyes had yet to slow. The two older wolves were unconcerned by the loss of their youngest member, and they now had their parries down to a science. One lunged forward quickly followed by the other, the repeated motions pushing me back step by step until I nearly tripped over the stake holding up one corner of our tent.

I was being drawn away from the larger battlefield, but there was nothing I could do to prevent the herding action. Not while I remained unwilling to outright slaughter my enemies and not while the smooth operators dodged most of my blows anyway. In a two-against-one altercation, it seemed inevitable that I would eventually be ground down beneath their mechanical attacks until I was forced to mimic the enemy youngster's show of submission.

And then a huge, brindled wolf leapt out of the fog with a smaller animal at his heels. *Hunter and Lia.* The latter rubbed her cheek against the former's shoulder in a display of pack solidarity and Hunter spared one quick swipe of his tongue across Lia's left eye before getting down to business.

I caught my breath in surprise as Lia darted in alone. The teenager drew the attention of one of the males then danced away on light feet, leaving the enemy torn between turning back around to face me and lunging at the younger half-blood. And Hunter took advantage of the moment of hesitation, sliding in front of the outpack male and freezing him with a single glance.

Now my only remaining attacker turned to face the larger threat, leaving me unencumbered for the first time since the skirmish had begun. I spared a quick glance across the larger battlefield, realizing that the sounds of fighting had ceased everywhere except in my immediate vicinity. Ginger and Cinnamon were standing over a cowering, now-human teenager while Glen guarded six frozen shifters scattered across the campsite. The enemy was entirely present and accounted for.

Except for one last shifter who had been intent upon taking me down only seconds earlier. But even as I turned back around to face him, Lia was leaping astride the stranger's back, drawing his eyes unconsciously to those of Hunter, who had positioned himself just behind his opponent's left shoulder.

The final enemy went still and Lia pranced triumphantly atop his back for a long moment, her joy at pulling her own weight in a successful battle nearly palpable in the air. The half-blood was so pleased, in fact, that she raised her muzzle to the sky in preparation for an exuberant howl.

I hated to be the one throwing cold water on the youngster's elation, but there was still the cookie lady to consider. So I did my pack leader job and slapped the teenager down.

"*Lia,*" I said quietly but sternly. In her enthusiasm, the kid struggled against my compulsion for a moment. But then she leapt down and slunk toward me on her belly in a simple but effective werewolf apology.

"I understand," I soothed. And I did. It was invigorating to discover your strengths when you were a sixteen-year-old girl who had always in the past been the weakest wolf at the party. Lia's unlikely partnership with Hunter had not only saved our pack, it seemed to have given the timid teenager a new lease on life.

I, on the other hand, was exhausted both physically and mentally. Sure, we'd conquered the invaders without loss of life on either side. And I had a good feeling about our ability to wrest information out of the teenager now pinned beneath the trouble twins' paws.

But, unlike Lia, I'd only barely managed to hold my own even with the help of the heavy hunk of steel clenched between my intertwined fists.

As if the thought had released the last iota of control I possessed over my tired muscles, the tip of said sword fell to the ground with a thunk. This battle had made one thing clear at least. As a pack leader, I was worse than worthless. An alpha I was not.

CHAPTER 8

But an alpha I was determined to become. So I squashed my own angst and headed over to deal with the trouble twins and their captured prey.

In human form, the teenage boy looked even younger than Lia and I couldn't help feeling sorry for him as I took in his scratched skin and submissive posture. Still, it wouldn't do for me to appear soft, not when the prisoner's compatriots might pop back to life at any moment. We needed to extract any information we could and then hit the road without allowing the morning battle to resume. So I firmed up my resolve to act like a traditional pack leader, folding the gifted mantle back around me like a protective cloak.

Before I could do more than nudge Glen and Cinnamon toward breaking camp, though, pounding footsteps drew my gaze away from our prisoner. Quill was running flat out toward us, hair soaked and only pants in place. "What happened?" the cowboy shifter demanded as he took in the jumble of wolves and camping paraphernalia dotting the site.

Despite my best efforts to keep my weaker half asleep, surprise combined with morning-fuzz brain woke the inner beast. With her at the helm, our eyes skimmed briefly across our newest member's six-pack abs, following the line of hair at the bottom of his flat belly until it disappeared behind his massive cowboy buckle. Quill hadn't taken the time to don shoes, I saw, but he *had* cinched his belt shut.

Too bad. The male's physique was impressive even by werewolf standards.

Mirroring my wolf's appreciation of the man-candy before us, Ginger hummed her interest in the cowboy shifter's half-clad body. But Hunter was less impressed. The uber-alpha's growl was low but intense, raising hairs on the back of my neck and changing Quill's body language from concern to aggression. Just what I needed—a fight within our own ranks to complete our pre-breakfast exertions.

Figuring the trouble twin's avid admiration wasn't helping matters, I dealt with the most likely source of strife first. "Ginger, you can join Cinnamon with the packing," I said firmly. In response, the teenage wolf shot me a grumpy glance before stretching upwards onto two legs, losing fur and gaining human characteristics as she rose.

But even though she followed my order to the letter, I didn't miss the way Ginger jutted out her naked chest and brushed up against Quill despite having plenty of space to walk around. As usual, the twin was complying...albeit grudgingly.

I wasn't surprised by Ginger's flirtiness, nor was I surprised by the cowboy shifter's response. What red-blooded American male wouldn't glance down at the erect nipples grazing his bare chest? A smirk lit Quill's face, proving that he liked what he saw, and I could tell it took an effort for our newest pack mate to refrain from reaching out and touching the merchandise being put so boldly on display.

But that issue soon became irrelevant when an overwhelming aroma of rotten bananas filled the air. *Pop. Pop, pop. Pop, pop, pop, pop.*

The first wolf to reanimate was the one I'd fought against at the very end of our battle, but soon all seven beasts were once again set into motion. Only the boy crumpled at our feet remained still, and that was only due to Hunter's quick thinking rather than to his previous compulsion. Before I even realized what was happening, the uber-alpha had lunged forward to physically pin the teenager to the earth using the force of his front paws.

Which left one enemy on the ground...and seven standing against us.

"Shit." The word slipped out of my mouth without conscious volition, but I stood by the sentiment nonetheless. My clan hadn't done so badly in the preceding fight, but I had a feeling we'd fare much worse a second time around. After all, I'd just sent three of our crew away in human form, and they'd be hard-pressed to fight if forced to make a second rapid shift after such a short recovery period.

Plus, I'd made the beginner mistake of abandoning my sword on the ground where it fell, which left me entirely defenseless. *Some alpha I am.*

Hunter's growl ratcheted up another notch, and Lia's furry body pushed up against the uber-alpha's side to either give or receive comfort. Our odds of survival weren't good even if Quill turned out to be adept at speedy transformations, which was far from a given. My own pack mates had learned the trick from our previous bloodling alpha, but most shifters took quite a while to change shape even under the best of circumstances. With angry werewolves out for blood to distract him, Quill might not manage to shift at all.

As I wracked my brain to think of some weapon I'd forgotten, the seven outpack males moved in to form a ring around us, their gazes still intent upon me and Lia and seemingly uninterested in the teenager who lay in the dirt at our feet. I didn't dare to breathe, waiting for the other shoe to drop.

Then, as if at a hidden signal, all seven turned as a unit and padded away. A stalemate—much better than the outcome I would have expected.

In fact, as the last furry tail disappeared into the rising mist, I had the surreal impression that our enemies had never actually been present in the flesh. Only the rotten-banana aroma—and the wild-eyed prisoner—proved that the preceding battle had actually occurred.

"Hunter...?" I wanted to ask him to see our enemies to the virtual door and ensure they didn't circle back around to ambush us before we were able to make tracks. But even I didn't have the guts to order an uber-alpha to do my bidding.

The strong shifter vacillated for a moment, his head whipping back and forth between the trees to the right and Lia to his left. At first, I thought my so-called mate had taken offense at even the carefully veiled command. But now I realized that Hunter simply felt uncomfortable relinquishing his ability to protect the girl with whom he seemed to have formed a battlefield attachment.

I've got her, I wanted to say. But instead, I simply reached out and pulled Lia's furry body against my legs. And as if he understood my unspoken words, Hunter nodded his thanks. Brushing past Quill in unconscious mimicry of Ginger's earlier actions, the uber-alpha provided a not-so-subtle warning to the cowboy shifter even as he headed off into the woods.

"Hey!" Quill complained as his legs were nearly thrust out from beneath him by the force of Hunter's passing. But I noticed that our newest pack mate didn't try to back his words up with a threat...which was a smart move. None of us mere mortals could hold a candle to Hunter's dominance. We were better off not even trying.

Then my attention returned to the prisoner, who was even now being pushed back toward the ground by Glen's human hands. "Don't even think about it," my beta growled. I wasn't so sure the kid had really been trying to escape. But a little intimidation never hurt in an interrogation setting, so I nodded my thanks before getting down to business.

"What's your name?" I asked, crouching down and pushing my upper body into the boy's personal space. He was still wearing the same sort of collar that had encircled each enemy werewolf's neck, and I could now pinpoint the rotten-banana odor that so recently filled the campsite. The source was apparently a small plastic cube embedded in the fabric, and as soon as my eye picked out the difference in texture, I reached forward to examine the device.

Before my fingers could even brush against his skin, though, the teenager cringed away as if I'd planned to either strike or strangle him. "Crew Franklin," he mumbled quickly in reply to my earlier question, and I could have sworn I saw a tear brimming up on the bottom lid of one eye.

I swore silently. The prisoner really was just a kid and one who probably hadn't learned to shift more than a few short months ago. He was fourteen, fifteen tops. Crew must have stumbled into outpack shenanigans way past his pay grade then gotten in over his head, but my gut told me he was still entirely redeemable. Given the right leadership, the boy would likely turn into a fine member of his own clan one day.

Not that I wanted the kid to know his interrogator was softening toward him. So I continued fumbling with the catch on his collar even as I bluffed using the deepest voice I could manage. "Okay, Crew," I said, stuffing the neckband in my pants pocket to be considered at a later date. "Here's how this is going to work. You're going to answer all of my questions without holding anything back. And if you tell me what I want to know, then I'll deliver you back to your father to be dealt with as he sees fit.

"On the other hand," I threatened, glaring into his eyes, "if you think you can lie to me or omit any relevant.details.... Well, you saw that wolf who was just here. He's pretty hungry and he likes raw, red meat for breakfast. We're running low on supplies, so you're on the menu, if you get my gist."

Crew flinched and Lia snorted beside me. The latter didn't buy my tough-guy stance for a moment, but she also wasn't the teenager I was trying to impress.

"Okay, sure, yes," our prisoner babbled. "I'll tell you anything. But I don't know much. I haven't been sworn in yet, just went to a few meetings as Talon's recruit."

"Talon?" I asked, keeping my questions short and open-ended. The kid seemed more likely to spill relevant details if I didn't lead him too closely.

Sure enough, Crew's eyes only flitted across his captors' faces for a moment before he fell all over himself to tell me about a group of outpack males that met regularly at various bars around the region. He didn't know anyone's last name, and I wasn't entirely confident that even the first names he spewed out were real. Still, the purpose of the group was as clear as it was chilling.

"To pledge, you have to capture a halfie," the kid told me earnestly. "They're not really human," he rushed on by way of explanation. "Just unnatural animals. Filth."

Despite having shed fur some minutes ago, Glen still growled in response to the kid's words and his fingers tightened around Crew's shoulders. I wasn't terribly pleased with the boy's language either, but this was an information-gathering session only. So I shook my head in subtle rebuke. "And what do you do with the halfies you catch?" I prodded.

"I'm not sure." A line formed between Crew's eyebrows as if he hadn't given the question much thought. I suspected our prisoner had been recently drawn into the group by the enticing camaraderie offered by a cluster of outpack males and hadn't worried too much about the big picture as long as his social needs were met.

But the big picture was exactly what I was trying to suss out. "What's the organization called?" I demanded, not giving him time to fully catch his breath.

"SSS," Crew replied easily. "The Shifter Sanitation Society. We're cleaning up the region...."

And then Quill was pushing me to the side as a rifle shot cracked out, breaking the morning stillness. Glen dove atop Lia, protecting her body with his own even though I suspected that the shooter could as easily kill both as one.

Silently, I berated myself for not being more prepared. There was nothing wolf teeth and human sword could do against a sniper hidden by the encircling fog. Suddenly, our location at the far edge of the campground seemed more hindrance than help.

My muscles twitched, begging me to run for cover. But there was no point in moving. We'd present even larger targets if we straightened back up, and the thin metal of our car's frame likely wouldn't shield us from the bullet of a high-caliber rifle.

Plus, there didn't end up being any reason to flee after all. Because the sniper appeared to have gotten what he came for and then left as silently as he'd arrived. As we waited, muffling our harsh breathing against crossed arms, the birds once again began to sing and the campground's usual woodland tranquility sprang back to life.

Well, most of the campground resumed its normal life. Crew, on the other hand, had been shot square through the left side of his chest, the tiny entrance wound appearing inconsequential until I noticed the massive stain of blood soaking into the dirt beneath him. And when I pressed my fingers to the boy's throat, I found no pulse.

There was only one conclusion to be drawn. Someone hadn't wanted Crew to spill his guts, so they'd chosen a much more final route to their preferred destination. They'd spilled the last of his life's blood instead.

CHAPTER 9

"Such a waste," Glen murmured as he helped me heave Crew's body onto the tent fly that was protecting the carpet beneath our car's hatchback. I pursed my lips and nodded but didn't say anything else. My beta understood that I was as torn up about the boy's death as he was, but we also needed to make good on our escape before anyone else was shot.

The only reason we hadn't left already, in fact, was because Hunter was still out there. I hoped he was following my orders and patrolling the boundaries of the campground for lingering enemy shifters. But I feared the elusive uber-alpha had instead been sucked into the drama and was even now lying wounded on the forest floor.

On the other hand, I could tell the trouble twins had a different notion entirely. They were convinced that the uber-alpha *was* the sniper.

So when the wolf we were all waiting for stepped into the clearing, Ginger and Cinnamon started toward him on lupine feet with lips curled. They'd shifted again too soon and would almost certainly be no match for the stronger werewolf as a result, but the duo were always up for a good brawl. Plus, they were expert bluffers and were used to harvesting the expected results from a show of strength.

To his credit, Hunter immediately abandoned the form in which he both felt more comfortable and harnessed greater offensive power, spreading his empty hands out to his sides in surrender as soon as he'd shifted. But the two-legger body language stopped there. Despite lacking canine sense organs, the uber-alpha raised his chin and sniffed the air like a dog as he entered our campsite. Then he blanched. "Who's hurt?" he demanded, gaze flicking across my pack mates as if he were counting heads.

If Hunter really is the sniper, he's even better at dissembling than the trouble twins are, I thought. But all I said was: "Walk with me."

Behind my back, the siblings growled their annoyance. But I ignored them and grabbed the uber-alpha's hand to pull him back in the direction from which he'd come.

Hunter's palm was warm and dry, albeit dirty from its recent contact with the earth. And, despite myself, I allowed my shoulder to drift closer to my companion's, my stride lengthening to match his even as the uber-alpha's steps slowed to make his pace more compatible with my shorter legs.

We fit, whispered the wolf who I'd thought was completely comatose within my human body. *Shh*, I reprimanded her. But I couldn't quite muster the energy to knock her all the way down. Good thing my animal half was too submissive to chafe against even a mild rebuke since I was nearly at the end of my rope.

"Who?" Hunter asked again, and the sound of his voice sent a tremor of excitement sparking down my spine. We were far enough away from my pack now that no one would know what we said if we spoke softly, and for an instant I imagined asking Hunter about his past. Was I right in thinking that he felt the same protectiveness toward Lia that I'd heard in his voice when he spoke of Daisy Rambler? What aspect of his childhood or youth, I wondered, had given him this unconventional soft spot for a downtrodden halfie?

I shook my head to clear it and promised myself a nap as soon as we were back on the road. I was drifting far off course and needed to answer the uber-alpha's question rather than peppering him with an interrogation of my own. So I forced the image of Crew's lifeless face to rise up behind my eyes, and the memory certainly did the trick of squashing my raging hormones.

As a result, my voice was terse when I spoke at last. "You smelled Crew —our captured enemy," I answered. "Someone shot him from the woods while you were gone. He's dead."

To my dismay, the uber-alpha appeared entirely unconcerned about the kid's demise. Instead, he was all business as he confirmed: "I heard the shot."

I drew in a breath to demand more information, but my companion was way ahead of me. Rubbing his thumb across my palm, he elaborated: "I didn't find the sniper, though. He was long gone, and so were the rest of the wolves. They'd parked half a mile away, on the other side of the campground."

The image of Crew's dead body stretched out beside my own flickered into my vision once again, making my stomach churn. I forced down a sour taste that threatened to expel yesterday's dinner, and the reaction wasn't entirely due to the memory either. Instead, Hunter's lack of interest in the boy's fate hurt nearly as much as Crew's death.

I loosened my fingers and disentangled my hand from the grasp of the uber-alpha who suddenly seemed more like a Tribunal enforcer than like my mate. Or I *tried* to. In the end, I was forced to jerk free of my companion's strong grip when he refused to let them go.

What did I do now? The words might as well have been written across the uber-alpha's face, and I almost laughed at his confusion. Much as it hurt, though, I was glad of the reminder that Hunter was uninterested in being part of a shifter pack. Given my weakness as an alpha, we couldn't afford to incorporate such a strong presence into our little band if he wasn't trustworthy beyond a shadow of a doubt.

"We're going to deliver Crew's body back to his family," I said instead of delving into the feelings that were best not dumped onto a stranger's shoulders. I swallowed, imagining having to tell the boy's family how and why he'd perished. I'd only known Crew for a few minutes, but I still felt like the teenager's death was my own fault.

"I can call someone from the Tribunal to come and pick him up if you'd rather," Hunter rumbled, patting at his bare ass as if a cell phone might materialize there if he looked hard enough. Despite myself, I sneaked a glance at the buttocks in question. Yep, Hunter's physique was even more impressive than Quill's.

Irrelevant, I reminded myself. But I still offered the uber-alpha my cell phone as a sort of consolation prize.

"Delivering Crew's body is no problem," I said before Hunter could dial. "But you won't fit into our car any longer. So if you want to call someone to pick you up...."

My words trailed off and I looked away, unable to meet Hunter's eyes as I summarily ejected him from our little clan. I didn't know whether the uber-alpha wanted to travel with us in the first place, and it had only been an hour since my pack mates had near-unanimously cast him out of our group without even needing my vote to clinch the deal. Still, I felt guilty to be the bearer of bad tidings.

To my surprise, Hunter touched my shoulder so briefly I almost thought I'd imagined it. Was *he* trying to console *me?* But then the uber-alpha had turned away, the phone raised to his ear as he relayed information about the battle just past.

I listened unabashedly, and my heart sank as I did so. Because it appeared we weren't the only halfies who had been attacked this morning. There was now another girl missing. And if Daisy Rambler's fate was any indication, this new kidnapping victim didn't have much time left to live.

***

"Serene," Ginger offered from the back seat half an hour after we'd pulled out of the campground with Quill, but not Hunter, in tow.

We were trying to come up with an honest yet complimentary review of the campground to thank the cookie lady for her midnight snack, but the trouble twin's word didn't quite match the reality of our experience. After all, while our head count remained the same as when we'd arrived at The Woodland Hideaway, Hunter's absence felt like the cavity left by a missing tooth—minor in reality but absurdly large when I poked at the space with my tongue.

Plus, our newest co-traveler was dead. Which I guess made him technically calm and tranquil. Still, death wasn't what I'd normally call serene.

"Pastoral," Cinnamon agreed. "The perfect vacation."

"Great wildlife sightings," Lia chimed in. And despite Crew's corpse acting like an anchor depressing my mood, I couldn't help laughing as every other member of the car cracked up at the girl's pun. Lia had definitely hit the nail on the head, so I obediently keyed her words into the review site and hit *Submit.*

The humor was much appreciated because we were even now turning through the ungated archway of the Franklin compound. The ostentatious entrance looked ominous and I had a feeling laughter would be hard to come by in the near future. I just hoped Crew's former pack leader wouldn't literally rip my head off for returning his underling in a homemade body bag.

Sure enough, our tires had barely crunched across five feet of gravel driveway when a man and two wolves stepped out of the trees and into our path. We weren't moving very fast, but Glen still had to slam on the brakes to prevent our car from sliding into the welcoming party, and Ginger growled quietly at the Franklins' cheek.

"Let's all be on our best behavior," I admonished the pack in general, seeking out the female trouble twin's gaze in particular. The redhead rolled her eyes, but nodded. She knew as well as I did that coming into another clan's territory with a bad attitude was a recipe for never leaving that territory alive.

"Shall I?" Glen asked, his hand on the door latch. But I shook my head. Despite my weak wolf, I was the pack leader and needed to act my part.

So I emerged from our vehicle alone and strode over to greet the older man, who I guessed had to be the Franklin alpha. From the stony expression on his face, I figured he was throwing some sort of compulsion in my direction, too. But my wolf was sound asleep and I couldn't even feel his power rolling off my back.

"Hunter said you'd be expecting me," I said rather than commenting on the silent contest that I'd won by dint of simply ignoring it. "I'm Fen."

The other pack leader didn't accept my proffered hand, nor did he offer his name. But the two wolves at his heels also didn't spring forward to rip out my throat, so I figured our introductions were a resounding success.

"You have our boy?" the two-legger demanded instead.

I pointed my chin toward the hatchback of the car, which Cinnamon was even now pushing open to reveal Crew's silent form. The boy's body was still warm, and I didn't blame the wolves on either side of me for growling as they caught the coppery scent of his blood.

Still, I couldn't let them get away with such an overt display of aggression either. So I stepped between my pack and the Franklin shifters, pulling my sword from its scabbard in one smooth arc. The sun gleamed on the polished metal blade and one of the pack leader's lackeys took an unconscious step backwards at the sight.

"Quaint," his alpha said shortly. "But you don't need that here. Your guardian made it entirely clear that every member of your little pack is under the protection of the Tribunal."

My guardian? I couldn't decide if the word sounded sweet...or paternalistic. So I ignored it just the way the Franklin alpha was ignoring my raised weapon and stepping around me to take in Crew's bloody corpse.

Despite his posturing and gruffness, I could tell the older man was honestly pained by the sight of his underling's body, so I met Glen's gaze across the car, beckoning my beta to join us in gently lifting the deceased down to the ground.

"He seemed like a good kid," I offered when the boy was once again laid flat on the earth. Soon, I knew, his pack would be lighting the traditional funereal bonfire, and I wished I could be present to speed him on his way into the afterlife. But, barring an invitation that I doubted would be forthcoming, I figured I should offer words of tribute now.

"My son was a strong hunter," the pack leader answered, making me start in surprise. Not because he'd turned the eulogy in a different direction. Unlike me, most werewolves would consider bravery more important to comment upon than personality. So the alpha's praise wasn't unexpected.

Instead, it was the word *son* that had caught my attention. I hadn't realized Crew was so highly ranked within the Franklin pack, and the boy's lineage made me wonder whether the SSS was more widely accepted than just being the renegade outpack organization I'd initially assumed.

No time like the present to test my hypothesis. "Crew was killed by the SSS," I offered now, keeping my attention trained on the other pack leader as I assessed his reaction.

If I'd hoped to startle a telling response out of the other alpha, I was disappointed. At first, he didn't even take his gaze away from his dead son's face. And when the pack leader did finally turn around to peer at me once again, the older man's expression was shuttered and impossible to read.

"Thank you for delivering my son," he said in a cordial but clear dismissal. The words were a slap in the face, a refusal to let us travel more than ten feet onto Franklin land after we'd done his pack a favor by delivering his son's dead body back into his loving arms.

But I could understand where he was coming from. We were an unknown entity. And I'd easily avoided the other shifter's compulsion, suggesting that I could out-alpha Crew's father in a fight.

True, that appearance was entirely incorrect. But the older pack leader didn't need to know that.

So I just shrugged and followed my friends back to our car. Still, as we made a three-point turn and exited the Franklin territory as quickly as we'd come, I realized that the other alpha had answered my question after all.

He'd never asked what "SSS" stood for. And, if the Franklin pack leader hadn't known, surely he would have requested more information about his son's murderers.

Which implicated the entire Franklin clan as potential members of the Shifter Sanitation Society.

CHAPTER 10

Outpack shifters seldom put down roots because most of us aren't strong enough to defend a permanent territory on our own. So I wasn't surprised to discover that Quill's home consisted of an old VW van currently parked in the bar's otherwise empty lot.

What did surprise me was the interior. The cowboy shifter had ripped out fake wood and vinyl and replaced the original seats and tables with custom-built furnishings that resembled a well-decorated if rather cramped apartment.

"Home sweet home," he said, spreading his hands wide in a rather self-conscious gesture of welcome as I followed him into the vehicle. I got the impression Quill thought I might judge the van lacking, but my pack and I had been bedding down together in a single tent for the better part of a month. An RV, even a homemade one, was a major step up.

"Impressive," I said, running one finger over a polished hardwood countertop. There wasn't even any dust present. But I guessed if you weren't part of a pack, there wasn't much to do with your free time other than clean.

Which reminded me of the shifters I was currently supposed to be managing. I poked my head back out the door just in time to catch Cinnamon bringing the two clips at one end of the jumper cables closer and closer together. Trust a trouble twin to think it would be interesting to see exactly what happens when you short out a car battery.

"*Cinnamon,*" I called, stopping him in the act. Then I shot a glance toward the empty building twenty feet away, hoping no one had heard me raise my voice. Shifter bars didn't tend to open until dusk, so we had several hours to get Quill's van back on the road before anyone else showed up.

Or at least I hoped that was the case. Still, I'd feel better once we'd left the scene of last night's mayhem behind.

"What?" the trouble twin asked, turning toward me. As he did so, his hands unconsciously drifted closer together and I winced, expecting to see sparks flying at any moment.

Then Lia had deftly removed the clips from Cinnamon's hands. The younger teenager shot me a comforting smile as she opened the front passenger-side door of the VW, adeptly swiveling the seat out of the way then snapping the jumper cables into place. "You can fire up our car now," she called softly to Cinnamon, who seemed a bit disappointed at having his toy taken away from him. Still, the easygoing shifter shrugged and obeyed.

"You'll keep an eye on him?" I asked Lia once Cinnamon was gone. It was common knowledge within our pack that the male trouble twin required constant human interaction if you didn't want to wind up in the middle of an intricately designed practical joke. His younger cousin was the mischief maker's designated babysitter this morning, and I hoped she was up to the job.

"Sure," Lia answered, gracing me with another gentle smile before she slipped away on near-silent feet.

My mouth quirked in a combination of pride and regret. Ever since this morning's battle, I'd noticed the girl's lupine half present behind her human eyes, giving Lia a dignity she hadn't previously possessed. As an alpha, it was immensely satisfying to see the two halves of an underling's personality growing together. As a halfie, though, I had to admit to being slightly jealous of the ease with which Lia accepted her wolf.

Look, my own wolf said simply, reminding me that she wasn't quite asleep at that particular moment either. At her behest, I turned back around to find Quill subtly drifting into my personal space. He wasn't quite close enough that I could politely slap him down, but he was still a little nearer than I would have liked. So I took a step backwards and diverted whatever the cowboy shifter had been thinking about by launching into my prepared spiel.

"So, if you still want to travel with us, the pack voted you in," I told him. "It looks like you're doing better than we are, though. And I totally understand if you've changed your mind now that you've gotten to know us better. We can just jumpstart your van and send you on your way with thanks if you'd rather. No harm, no foul."

What I was saying without spelling it all the way out was that I wasn't going to be an asshole alpha about the whole thing if Quill had gotten cold feet after witnessing our defeat this morning. Pack leaders tended to be possessive of their manpower, unwilling to let anyone who'd sworn to their clan go without a fight. But I didn't have the lupine dominance to back up that stance even if I'd wanted to.

Another thing Quill doesn't really need to know about us.

"No, I'm in," the cowboy shifter said almost too quickly. I cocked my head in consideration. Maybe he was lonelier than he looked—it *was* hard for our lupine natures to handle life outside a pack.

Or maybe there was something else going on.

"I noticed the way you looked at Ginger this morning," I prodded. "She's a bit of a tease...." Then I smothered a smile as the strong, buff cowboy shifter blushed bright red and averted his eyes.

"Would you mind...?" he started, then tried a different tack. "Is she available?"

Well, it looked like Ginger's flirtations were good for something after all if they were going to win a strong shifter like Quill over to our side. Still, I didn't want him thinking the trouble twin was a foretold benefit of joining our pack.

"She *is* available," I answered carefully. "But this isn't the kind of clan where a pack leader's permission holds any sway over who the members of that pack date. And Ginger seems to be having a lot of fun playing the field at the moment."

I didn't know how else to warn our newest member that the female trouble twin was likely to love him and leave him. After all, I didn't want to actually call my friend a slut because she really wasn't. If Ginger had a theme song, it would be *Girls just want to have fun*. She never overtly promised anything she didn't plan to deliver.

"Fair enough," Quill answered. "I just...."

Before he could go on, though, my phone chimed and I held up one finger to pause our conversation. I wasn't usually so rude, but Ginger and Glen were guarding the perimeter while also doing their best to leverage their online savvy to determine the identity of the halfie girl who had so recently been kidnapped. If anything showed on either search, I wanted to know about it right away.

Sure enough, Ginger had texted me an update on her investigation: *Girl is Savannah Abrams. Mother willing to talk to us this evening. Come to dinner, stay the night, she says. Yes/no?*

The twin had included an address about two hundred miles distant. That should give us just enough time to hunt down some lunch to round out this morning's granola bars and beef jerky before hitting the highway.

And if Mrs. Abrams lived east of here...well, I hadn't actually promised Hunter that I'd head west, now had I?

Yes. Thx, I keyed in quickly before turning back to my current companion with an apology on my lips.

Once again, the cowboy shifter had drifted closer, this time so he could peer over my shoulder. "Anything important?" he asked, and I angled the phone so he could read Ginger's words. Quill's manners seemed a little less polished this morning than they had been the night before, but there was no point in keeping him in the dark since he'd know our itinerary soon enough anyway.

"This is the halfie girl Hunter mentioned?" Quill asked after he'd read our exchange. When I nodded, he paused as if unsure how to word his next question.

I had a feeling I knew what was on his mind, so I nudged him a little. "Spit it out," I said. "You aren't going to offend me." I'd had fun forcing Hunter to stumble over his verbal feet around my half-blood heritage, but Quill seemed like a nice guy who just wasn't sure what to say without raising my hackles. So I gave him the benefit of the doubt.

"Is this whole pack...? Well, I mean, I know you and Lia are half-werewolves," Quill said, "but I couldn't tell about everyone else. Is that what you all have in common?"

Nicely said. But while I could appreciate the cowboy shifter's careful wording, his question didn't entirely make sense. "You know a guy can't really be a halfie, right?" I asked. Then I clarified: "I mean, to get technical on you, werewolfism is an X-linked, dominant trait. So guys either are shifters or they aren't. Doesn't matter who their parents are once they pass puberty and prove they can change forms. It's just female half-bloods who give birth to human children and show hybrid characteristics."

"Well, yeah, but...."

I could tell Quill was more of the school of thought that anyone whose parents weren't both 100% shifter was a halfie. Among his friends, he probably called humans "meat" too.

The old-fashioned sentiments annoyed me, but they were understandable since most shifters felt the same way. *Not a deal breaker for him joining our pack*, I told myself. After all, everyone was a creature of their environment and anyone could be taught.

So I gave Quill what he wanted to know. "No, Glen's a pure-blood," I told him. "And even though you wouldn't believe it from watching his antics, Cinnamon can trace his ancestry back to the first wolf, or close to it. Which makes Ginger a pure pack princess, of course."

Then I decided I might as well push a little further. After all, I'd answered Quill's nosy question, which made this a perfect opportunity for a not-so-polite query of my own. "So what's the deal with you being in outpack territory anyway?" I continued before the cowboy shifter could derail the conversation. "You seem like a nice guy, a strong shifter; any pack would be lucky to have you. Why wander the cold outside world with the rest of us?"

For a moment, I thought Quill wouldn't answer. Then his eyes took on a faraway cast and his lips turned down into an expression of pure melancholy. "My mate," he said finally, and I could easily fill in the blanks as the story tumbled off his lips in stops and starts.

The parts he left out were simple to guess because I'd heard the same tale many times before. Werewolf packs made for lots of Romeo-and-Juliet unions—either you fell in love with a mate in an enemy clan or you ached for someone too far above or below your own station for your alpha to approve the union. Some shifters sucked it up and did whatever their leader told them to, accepting a second-best spouse. Others—like Quill, apparently —eloped, dreaming that they'd be able to carve out a place for themselves beyond the borders of sanctioned pack territories.

"But it was a stupid move," the cowboy shifter finished. "Faye's brothers caught up with us before we'd been outpack for three weeks. I thought the worst they'd do was rip her away from me, which would have been bad enough. But they decided to make an example of their own sister instead."

He paused, and turned away, probably fighting the tears I'd seen welling up in his eyes at the memory. And I immediately felt like an asshole for making him relive the experience. Still, if Quill was joining our little clan, then I needed to know what kind of dangers were coming along on his coattails.

So I prodded my companion's tale along when the history lesson appeared to have petered out. "What happened?"

"I wasn't strong enough to protect her," the cowboy shifter replied, squaring his shoulders and looking me straight in the eyes this time around. "They pushed me aside and leaped on their own flesh and blood in wolf form...." His words trailed off and he gulped back a sob.

"They killed her," I murmured. It was a terrible story with a predictable ending, but the upshot was actually good for our pack. If Faye's brothers had taken their revenge, then they wouldn't be out pounding the pavement in an attempt to take Quill down. We could safely give the cowboy shifter a home in our transient pack without worrying that his not-quite-in-laws would come slavering for our blood as well.

"Yeah," my companion confirmed in a whisper. "They killed her." He closed his eyes and took a deep breath, and when he spoke his words were once again firm and easy to hear. "But I'm not going to let that happen a second time. If I find another mate—or even if I don't—I'll be strong enough to protect the people I care about."

I won't let you down. The words hung in the air, unsaid but implied. And if I'd had any doubts about letting Quill into our clan in the past, the misgivings were washed away in the face of his selflessness and confidence.

The trouble was, I wasn't nearly as confident that I'd be able to protect the pack Quill was becoming a part of. And, as an alpha, that responsibility rested firmly on my shoulders.

CHAPTER 11

"Deer for lunch *again?*" Ginger grumbled. Still, she was the first to shed her human clothes as we tumbled out of our two vehicles in the secluded pull-off a few miles into the national forest.

Of course, the trouble twin's alacrity at disrobing might have been due to enthusiasm at the opportunity to parade around naked in front of our pack's newest member once again rather than excitement at the prospect of yet another catch-your-own dinner. But who was I to complain about someone else's overactive hormones when I couldn't seem to get that absent uber-alpha's amber eyes out of my mind?

Ginger appeared to be better at attracting her intended quarry than I was because Quill's gaze immediately drifted south, caressing the trouble twin's curvy form. But her prey's attention didn't remain riveted for more than a moment before he returned to fidgeting with the cell phone in his pocket.

"Are you sure we shouldn't just stop at a sit-down restaurant along the way so we can get to our destination faster?" Quill asked after a moment of strained silence. "My treat."

The rest of the pack paused in their pre-shift preparations, hungry eyes flicking between our newest member and my indecisive face. Their wolves were all wide awake now, and I saw Cinnamon lick his lips in an almost lupine gesture of anticipation. The trouble twin would be thrilled at the opportunity to order meat that came skinned and deboned, and I couldn't really say I didn't feel the same way. On the other hand, Quill had no idea how much food five young-adult shifters could eat if he thought his funds would hold up to many restaurant outings for the entire pack.

"That's nice of you to offer," I said, letting him down gently. "But it's probably better to save that nest egg for when we really need it. Plus, look," I added, gesturing at the nearby trees that displayed a browse line of absent greenery for the first six feet above the ground. "Any biologist will tell you that we're doing our civic duty by filling in for absent predators and culling the local deer herd."

"Yeah, that's us, always looking out for the greater good," Ginger murmured. I could tell she was more annoyed at Quill's lack of attention to her naked body than at the lost restaurant opportunity, though, and I resolved to pull the young woman aside later and let her know that our newest pack member had asked after her. I suspected the cowboy shifter's current lack of interest was just due to discomfort as he tried to fit into a new group rather than to actual apathy toward the young woman's enticing assets.

But, for now, I decided it was better to get us all shifted and into the woods before the trouble twin in question got her panties into any more of a twist...and before a state trooper came along and decided to investigate

88

half a dozen naked young people standing by the side of the road. "Quill?" I asked when the cowboy shifter continued to hesitate.

"Just a minute," he said, averting his eyes in what might have been submission or was perhaps just continued discomfort. "I'd planned to meet up with a friend when we hit town and I need to push back our appointment...."

His voice trailed off and I shrugged. Hopefully whoever he was texting wouldn't be too annoyed at being blown off. No point in our newest member breaking off all ties with the outside world as he started a fresh existence as part of our pack.

He's not a perfect fit, my wolf whispered in the back of my mind, interrupting the moment. She seemed obsessed with square pegs and round holes these days, but I was less concerned than the wolf was about this slight chink in Quill's usually courtly armor. It wasn't as if the rest of my pack mates had instantly fallen into line when we set off on the road together either.

Just a week ago, in fact, Ginger had insisted in arguing against every single suggestion I made. And now...okay, so the trouble twin still argued against every suggestion I made. But I'd gotten used to her quirks, just as Quill would get used to the workings of our found family. My comrades and I weren't quite as civilized as the average werewolf clan, maybe, but we had each other's backs.

The thought prompted me to scan the parking area and check on the state of everyone else's shifts. As young as Lia was and a halfie to boot, it wouldn't have surprised me if the girl needed help with her second human-to-wolf transformation of the day. But the kid seemed to be doing okay, even though she'd staked out a spot on the far side of the car rather than joining the rest of us in our little huddle.

I raised my eyebrows in question as I watched the naked girl slowly sprout fur. In reply, she shot a glance toward Quill by way of explanation. Yeah, the teenager probably had a point, I thought as I pursed my lips and nodded. No reason to flaunt her nubile but unavailable body in front of a shifter who hadn't yet entirely fallen in with our pack's casual approach toward nudity.

Speaking of casual, there was such a thing as being *too* casual. Ginger —who I knew for a fact could shift at the drop of a hat—was still hovering a hair's breadth away from the cowboy shifter, her two-legged form twisting and turning as she tried in vain to capture the latter's attention.

I rolled my eyes and removed the sword I'd been wearing ever since that morning's altercation, stuffing the sheathed weapon behind the back seat for safekeeping. I felt oddly naked without the blade, my still-present clothes making no impression when I lacked anything pointy and sharp with which to defend myself.

You have me, promised my wolf, wide awake now that the prospect of finally donning her favored fur form was at hand.

Sure, I soothed her. Like every other shifter, I felt the pull of being four-legged deep within my bones after staying human for so long. But in my case, the attraction was always tempered by the reality of being saddled with a woefully weak wolf.

Our pack is strong, my wolf promised me. *And I'll do whatever you say.*

Of course she'd do what I said. That was the entire problem with our partnership in a nutshell—lack of leadership potential on the wolf's part.

Still, I quickly kicked off my shoes, then folded jeans and undies and tossed the whole pile of clothing onto the back seat with the rest of my pack's apparel. Finally, taking a deep breath, I rejoined the other shifters— half of us already four-legged and the rest, even Quill, now naked.

Everyone except Ginger appeared calm and collected as the onset of our hunt rapidly approached. Lia had padded around to join us and was now tussling with Cinnamon on the ground, the larger wolf letting our youngest member win despite her youthful lack of muscles. In contrast,

Glen stood poised in lupine form, waiting for Quill to fall onto four legs before he relaxed his guard.

And Ginger...Ginger was advancing on me with eyes flashing even as she slid covert glances at the cowboy shifter. The latter still hadn't properly admired her visible assets and was instead watching me with hungry eyes, a definite slight that I knew the young woman wouldn't let slide.

I saw the attack coming before she launched herself forward, but I misgauged the volatile redhead's intentions. By the glint in her eye, I'd assumed she was pissed and needed a cat fight to get it out of her system. So I raised both hands to repel her imminent strike.

But Ginger didn't hit me. Or, rather, she *did* let her body slam into mine, pressing my bare butt up against the warm metal of the car door.

On the other hand, the trouble twin didn't intend to cause harm. Instead, the slightly taller woman dipped her neck even as she pushed my chin upwards by cradling the back of my head with two firm hands.

Then she pulled me into a deep, uninhibited kiss.

***

For a split second, I imagined that Hunter was the one merging his lips with mine. The uber-alpha would taste just the way he smelled—like cold root beer, the refreshing aroma enveloping me and beating back the summer heat. I'd kiss him back....

I opened my eyes and pushed Ginger away as I regained my senses. "What the heck, Ginger?"

The trouble twin's cheeks were flushed, and I expected her to shoot another pointed glance at Quill. After all, my friend had gone for a classic catch-the-guy's-attention move and would be wanting to know if her girl kiss had paid off.

But instead, my pack mate just gazed into my eyes, searching my face as if trying to decide whether the lipstick she'd smeared onto my skin suited my complexion. I wiped the goop away in disgust. It was bad enough to watch Quill and Ginger tiptoeing around each other without being caught in the middle of their mating dance.

"Just a good-luck kiss," she said after a moment, and I caught a flash of something I couldn't quite name in her eyes as she turned away. Cinnamon, ever alert to his sister's moods, scrambled out from beneath his cousin's furry body and trotted over to rub up against Ginger's bare leg in sympathy.

And then there were two reddish wolves on the ground instead of one, and Quill and I were the only humans left standing. "Let's hunt," I said curtly, still a bit annoyed at the trouble twin and concerned over the cowboy shifter's foot dragging.

But I didn't want to initiate my own shift with murky emotions at the forefront of my mind. So I took a deep breath just the way my previous alpha had taught me, then I relinquished human control for a split second.

I transformed as I fell forward, arms that would have kept me from hitting the ground becoming legs and my tail thrusting to one side to steady my descent. At the same time, the wolf brain rose up to take over our shared form—my least favorite part of the shifting process. This changing of the guard always felt like diving into a deep, frigid ocean, the chill making my bones ache and only slowly receding as I acclimated to the abrupt change in virtual temperature.

Our shared ears popped. Now I was entirely subsumed by the wolf, and for a split second I drifted in darkness. Then, desperately, I clawed my way upwards.

I'd made this journey many times before, but today the faint pinprick of light showing through the wolf's eyes seemed impossibly far away. In fact, I appeared to be falling deeper into the wolf's subconscious rather than rising to join her at the helm. *This is the shift where I lose my footing and drown,* I thought in dismay.

This type of slippage was normal the first few times a teenager tried to change forms, of course. But my transformations hadn't gotten any easier during the last seven years since I hit werewolf puberty.

Today's shift was the worst experience to date. Always in the past, I'd scrambled upwards as best I could, clawing my way through the wolf's throat with torn fingernails while hoping I'd make my way back into the light. And each time, I'd thought I'd failed before finally managing to emerge breathless back in the wolf's body.

This time, though, I was just so very tired. The hour was only a little past noon, but the day had already been long and the preceding night short. Quill's addition to our pack was a triumph, but the change in group dynamics left everyone off kilter and in need of a little extra alpha attention.

I barely felt up to the task.

Then there was the confusion of Hunter's sudden presence and equally sudden absence. My stalker had dropped his verbal bomb last night, throwing out the M word as if "mate" wasn't an expletive in my lexicon. And, yes, I'd been too chicken shit to call him on it. But did Hunter *have* to find it so easy to hare off in search of another halfie girl this morning with barely a word of farewell?

No matter the reason, I had a sinking suspicion that this was the time I wouldn't make it back into human form at the end of my shift. I'd already spent way too long down in the wolf's belly, drifting further into her virtual intestines with every second as if my struggles were mired down by quicksand designed to pull me under and keep me there.

My pack mates would be wondering why the wolf was frozen in place, but I could neither hear them nor feel their furry bodies nudging against my shoulder. And without the presence of my clan, I wasn't so sure I cared that my heavy eyelids were drifting closed. A little nap was called for....

And then the wolf brain was beneath my human mind, pushing me gently but firmly upwards until I could share the view from behind her lupine eyes. Within our corporeal body, she licked me in welcome and my human mind covered virtual face with ethereal hands in order to repel her advances. As usual, the wolf was absurdly happy to see me, as if I wasn't always present, always in control of our shared body even when we donned fur.

Well, as long as I don't drown betwixt and between. I was ashamed of myself for wallowing in that moment of weakness, and I was probably more curt with the wolf than I should have been as a result. *Leave me alone*, I ordered, and her enthusiasm abruptly waned.

Now the captain of our shared ship, I dropped into downward-facing dog to stretch our four-legger body and relax our spine. Then I glanced back over one shoulder to make sure Quill had followed suit. Sure enough, our newest pack mate had nearly achieved lupine splendor, although he was taking even longer than me to get his feet solidly beneath him.

Everyone else, though, schooled by our old alpha, was surefooted and ready to run. And I realized that I wasn't quite ready for Quill to understand our strange lupine dynamics anyway, to figure out that the alpha werewolf who he'd agree to answer to was actually the weakest one in the pack.

So I raised my chin to the sky and let my wolf howl out her joy at finally being surrounded by her favorite furry companions once more. Then the five of us loped forward, Quill trailing a full measure behind.

CHAPTER 12

Ginger took the lead, her stronger wolf easily picking up a scent that the rest of us had missed. Nose to the earth, she startled the first deer within minutes.

But our potential prey was protecting two young fawns that must have been born later than the usual season. The flanks of the spindly-legged youngsters were still dappled with sun spots, and I shook my head in negation when the trouble twin glanced back at me in question. If we'd been starving, our pack could have easily taken down either the doe or the fawns or both. But there was no point in breaking up a family unit when the six of us were just having a little fun and seeking to ease average daily hunger pangs.

Glen must have predicted my response and peeled away from our group moments earlier because I now heard him yipping news of yet another find off to our left. I sniffed at the air, trying to grab hold of the pack bond that kept alphas apprised of each shifter's whereabouts and emotions. But the subtle web of connection that my newfound alpha abilities should have created instead eluded my fingertips and disappeared like a dream upon waking—one moment the knowledge was so vivid I felt as if I could step out into it; the next moment the vision might never have existed.

Not quite right, my wolf whispered, trying her best to be helpful. But I didn't need to be told that my inability to control the pack bond wasn't quite right. It was all part and parcel of having pack-leader status thrust upon me by another rather than growing gradually into organic strengths that had always been part of my DNA.

Shh, I admonished my inner beast yet again rather than trying to explain away my frustration. At least I could still use the information gleaned by my more ordinary senses even though the pack bond was missing in action. So I squashed my inner turmoil and turned to lead the other four wolves in the direction from which Glen's call had most recently emanated.

The pack was unaware of my newest failure, so they continued to show off the usual high spirits of a joint hunt. Or perhaps I should say the *excessively* high spirits. Because as Ginger and Cinnamon bounced past, I saw that his ear had already ended up between her sharp teeth and bloodshed appeared imminent.

Just what we need, I thought. *Another case of pack mates injured by friendly fire.*

Figuring I might as well save Cinnamon's skin while I had the opportunity, I pushed a little more spring into my step and knocked up against Ginger's hip in warning. *Cool it*, I thought, making my intentions clear by the tilt of my neck and the slight erection of hairs on my ruff.

Sure enough, the female trouble twin released her brother as soon as she caught my eye. But that didn't mean she was happy about being chastened. Instead, the pack princess growled at me, her rampant wolf easily able to tell that it surpassed the strength of my own measly animal now that we were both four-legged.

I probably should have slapped her down with what little alpha dominance I did possess. After all, not even the most easygoing pack leader would allow an underling to get away with such an obvious display of insolence.

But, if push comes to shove, do I have the teeth to back up my demands? The answer was a resounding "no," so I instead turned away to peer over one shoulder at the final members of our little band.

At least something was going right today. I was glad to see that Quill had taken the time to insinuate his way into Lia's good graces, she being the only member of our pack who had wanted the cowboy shifter gone. The young female still seemed uncertain about her current partner's intentions, but she was at least willing to run side by side with his larger masculine form as long as the rest of the clan was nearby. *Making progress.*

The pack bond... my wolf whispered again, interrupting my thoughts. This time my silent snarl made her drop all control over our shared body and we tumbled face first into the leaves. *Great.* I'd startled the beast out of her sole job—keeping our joint body moving forward.

Do I have to do everything around here? I grumbled, pushing through the fog that lay between human brain and animal body to get our muscular system in order once again.

I felt a little bad about the slap down, though, so I tried to explain myself to my alter-ego as we once again trotted forward to rejoin our companions. *Now isn't the time to figure out the pack bond,* I told her. *Now is the time to hunt.*

My inner wolf didn't respond, a gaping hole instead appearing within our shared body where her consciousness had existed only a moment before. But I shrugged away her absence. Instead, I focused on catching my stride before looking forward to where Quill and Lia had surged past while I was getting my lupine body back in order.

Like the trouble twins, this other duo was also rushing toward Glen's most recent beckoning bark. But Lia had slowed her steps and glanced backwards to check on me as she ran past.

So I saw pain fill the youngster's eyes as she yelped and danced sideways, holding one forefoot up as blood streamed down from cut pad to forest floor. And for an instant I felt her agony...agony that had resulted directly from my own inattention to pack duties.

My own inner conversation combined with the girl's natural empathy had taken my friend's attention away from her surroundings just long enough for the forest to intervene. And nature, as always, was red in both tooth and claw.

***

Pain and surprise immediately prompted Lia to initiate a shift into her more familiar form. But I knew such a transformation would be a mistake. Sure, the girl would feel more comfortable as a human, but hopping half a mile on one leg is much harder than limping out of the woods on three paws. Plus, if Lia shifted to two feet, another transformation into fur form was unlikely to happen today.

Time to stop this change before it really begins. More harshly than I would have liked, I grabbed the young wolf's ruff between my lupine teeth then shook firmly enough to garner her full attention.

As I did so, I saw human rationality slowly seeping back into Lia's eyes, overcoming the wolf's instinctive response to pain. Meanwhile, the electricity of impending transformation began ebbing out of the air around us both.

For a long moment, Lia remained poised between two forms. But then she nodded, a two-legger gesture that sat strangely upon her lupine form but that eased my worries and doubts. The girl had gotten a handle on her urge to shift and would stay four-legged for the foreseeable future.

Releasing a sigh of relief, I glanced around us at a forest gone suddenly quiet. We'd been at the tail end of the pack when Lia cut her paw, so no one else had noticed our absence as they bounded forward in search of Glen's chosen prey. But despite the fact that my companion and I were now entirely alone in the woods, I knew precisely where our pack mates were located. Because, after fumbling at an elusive connection for the last month, the pack bond had finally clicked into place without any effort on my part.

As a result, I could feel but not see Ginger and Glen leap for a yearling doe's jugular. And I could feel but not see Cinnamon and Quill yapping at the prey's heels. All four were excited and enjoying the hunt, although my secondhand experience of their reality was entirely different from their own. Instead of reveling in an imminent triumph, in fact, I found myself lost in the encompassing darkness of the other wolves' bellies.

Dark, close, cold.

Claustrophobia nearly sent me reeling back into my own skin. But I didn't want to leave an injured Lia alone in the forest while I disappeared on lupine feet in search of aid. And there was no need to abandon her, even momentarily, because my alpha senses were already in contact with the rest of my pack. I just needed to claw my way up out of their bellies in order to get their attention.

Cinnamon, the weakest wolf, was also the easiest to overcome with my alpha compulsion. Using far less effort than I'd expended entering my own lupine body thirty minutes earlier, I now found myself looking out through the male trouble twin's eyes. Sunlight streamed down through a gap in the canopy, warming our shared hide, and his body's adrenaline made my own heart pump faster in sympathy.

From my safe perch behind Cinnamon's eyes, in fact, I could see for the first time that the male was tethered to his sister just as firmly as I was to any of my pack mates. The ethereal rope shone visibly in the air between the two, a tightrope my alpha sense could easily walk across.

As quickly as the impulse entered my mind, I found myself bridging the minds of two pack mates rather than just one. So when Ginger's teeth ripped through tough deer hide, Cinnamon and I both tasted the salty blood in our mouths and we both felt her triumph at yet another successful hunt.

Helpful, I thought. I hadn't meant to cast the words out across the pack bond, but the male trouble twin jolted as if I'd spoken in his ear. Even Ginger flinched to peer back over one shoulder, ears pinned in confusion.

My hold over Glen was considerably weaker than my connection to Cinnamon due to the former's greater dominance, but my second in command still understood what was going on more quickly than the others. He stepped away from the dying deer and lifted his chin to the sky in a howl that pulled the other three shifters to his side in an instant. He—and I by proxy—now had their complete attention.

I wasn't sure how long our nebulous connection would last, though. So I got down to business right away. Pulling gently away from the pack bond, I left the line open as if turning my cell to speaker phone. I could listen and speak to my pack still, but now I could also focus on the real world beneath my lupine paws.

Lia was panting beside me, I—and the rest of the pack—now saw. Blood flowed copiously from her damaged foot, and I licked the gash clean with my tongue.

The gesture transferred down the tether just as effectively as my spoken word had a moment earlier. And as Glen and the trouble twins looked through my eyes at the wounded wolf lying in front of me, their anguish amplified my own. For a moment, our shared emotions bounced back and forth between us in a feedback loop that seemed poised to knock us all off our feet.

Then my wolf was present once more, easing the pack's heartache by the simple refusal to take part. She shuffled her paws against the leaf mold and in the process channeled our worry into the soil beneath our feet. *Shh,* she whispered at last, this final sound for me alone rather than transmitting to the entire pack.

The wolf was right. We'd get nowhere by drowning in Lia's misery. So I took a deep breath, re-centered myself, and found I was able to slim our communication line down to simple human language. *Lia cut her foot,* I explained, the distancing effect of words relieving some of our shared unease.

Unfortunately, my focus on the girl pulled her into the pack bond along with the rest of us. Momentarily, Lia's pain flared through our shared connection once again, but this time we felt the agony within our own bodies. As a unit, each of us raised our right front feet off the ground in sympathy.

Through Glen's eyes, I could see Quill cocking his head to one side quizzically. Only then did I realize that the cowboy shifter had been absent from our previous communication. No big surprise since he'd only been a member of our clan for less than a day.

But I didn't want our pack divided. So I thrust forth feelers that, once connected, yanked the final member of our clan into our shared consciousness.

Quill took in the situation quickly and showed his mettle by managing to send words down the invisible tether just as I had. *I'll walk Lia back to the cars,* he offered. The words were excessively loud, as if our newest pack mate had put an inordinate amount of force behind the statement in order to be heard at all. But I was impressed nonetheless.

Lia was less thrilled, though. She winced, and this time I didn't think the reaction stemmed from her aching paw. So I shook my head and chose another pack mate instead. *Cinnamon,* I commanded simply.

The easygoing trouble twin took off toward us at a run as soon as he heard his name. Greenery seemed to whip past my nose even though my physical body told me I was standing still, and the strange combination of sensations made me sick to my stomach. I pulled back without meaning too, and suddenly the pack bond shattered around us with a jolt.

Streamers that had connected me to five other shifters moments earlier now flung back in my face as if a stretched rubber band had snapped. I cradled a suddenly aching head with two paws. *Ow,* I winced, glad I wasn't able to transmit this new misery to my fellows.

Or at least I hoped I hadn't. Luckily, when I finally managed to open my eyes, Lia was eying me quizzically, suggesting that I was the only one affected by the blow-back.

In a perfect world, I would have rekindled the pack bond in order to ask Lia how she was feeling. But the notion of trying to hook back into our previous linkage didn't seem very palatable at that moment. Instead, I simply licked her ears soothingly, and the gentle whimper of pain that had been threading out of the other wolf's throat for the last several minutes slowly ceased.

In fact, by the time Cinnamon arrived, his younger cousin was gamely standing on three legs, ready and willing to limp back toward our waiting vehicles. I made as if to go with them, but the trouble twin shot me a glance that clearly stated *I've got this covered.*

Then he gently nipped the end of Lia's tail, teasing her back into good spirits. Even my over-protective streak had to admit that our pack's youngest member was in good hands.

Or, rather, in good paws.

So I merely watched their retreating forms for a moment to make sure Lia would be able to handle the journey ahead. Then I whirled on my heel and ran flat out toward the pack with whom I suddenly shared an even stronger connection.

CHAPTER 13

We gorged on raw, dripping deer meat until we could barely move. And while my human brain found the feast distasteful, I had to admit that the uncooked flesh filled a void within my lupine body that had previously been gaping cavernously empty.

As a result, I expected my wolf brain to dance with satiated joy as our stomach finally reached full capacity. But the backlash from the broken pack bond had knocked her into silence instead.

While I licked my muzzle clean as best I could, I debated my wolfless state. Until recently, I'd generally figured a day without comments from the peanut gallery was a good day. And, from a more functional perspective, my animal half's current absence was actually a boon because it kept her submissive nature a secret from Quill for a little while longer at least. I trusted our newest pack mate, but I'd learned the hard way that a halfie could never be too careful about who she took all the way into her confidence.

Still, I missed the animal's gentle presence at the back of my mind. So I prodded gently at the hole she'd left behind, hoping my wolf would rise back up to greet me.

Nothing. Well, my animal half would return when she was good and ready. And, in the meantime, I should probably have been thinking about wounded Lia rather than about my sleeping wolf anyway.

If we take off now, I estimated, *our exuberant, newly fed animal bodies will likely reach the parking area just about when our injured member limps in on three legs. Perfect timing.*

We'd bandage the girl's wound in an effort to get by without stitches, then we'd make tracks toward Mrs. Abrams' promised hospitality. *And I can treat Cinnamon to that store-bought meal he's been hankering after while we're at it,* I thought with a smile. The trouble twin deserved a hamburger for being willing to forgo our recent feast in order to help his younger cousin out.

I yipped an order, and the three wolves currently clustered around the deer carcass came to attention in an instant. Together, we bounded away through the forest, soon hitting a broad human trail that I suspected would lead us directly back to the parking area where we'd left our vehicles.

Now that I'd started worrying about Lia, though, my earlier enjoyment of the day had fled. So I added a little extra speed to my already fleet feet and couldn't resist feeling along the pack bond in search of the girl's presence.

Or, rather, I couldn't resist stretching toward where my memory of the pack bond had once lain. Because, like my wolf, our pack's nebulous shared consciousness was now missing in action.

To sooth the ache resulting from suddenly being alone in my own head, I closed my eyes for a moment, soaking up the tranquility of the forest we were traveling through. It was easy to run blind along our current trail, and it felt good to stretch my senses to their limits. Even without my wolf lending her assistance, I could occasionally catch a whiff of Glen, Ginger, and Quill as they trotted along in my wake. High above our heads, a scarlet tanager sang his raspy tune, while below me...

...below me a warm but motionless body tumbled me out of my reverie and back into the present. I'd literally tripped over Cinnamon's prone form before I saw him. And when I looked down, I nearly lost my lunch.

The trouble twin's fur had turned a more rusty red than its usual ginger hue due to copious quantities of dried blood. Wounds dotted his body from head to tail, and the male who usually vibrated with energy and good humor was now as still as death.

For a gut-wrenching moment, in fact, I didn't think his wolf was even breathing. Immediately, my throat tightened in despair. *Lost....*

But, finally, Cinnamon's ribcage slowly rose and lowered, and my lungs mimicked the motion as I inhaled a gasping breath of air. Only then did I realize that I'd shifted back to human form without conscious volition and that a twig was sticking into my bare skin as I knelt by my injured pack mate's side. But I didn't move except to lean closer to the comatose wolf's warm body.

My brain was fuzzy from the shift, which might be why I couldn't quite figure out what had happened. Our attackers wouldn't have followed us all the way from the campground to this national forest, would they? But what else could have torn Cinnamon to shreds? A bear?

"Where's Lia?" Ginger pushed me out of the way and slapped her brother hard across his furry muzzle. Although her aggression wasn't aimed at me, the female trouble twin's actions jolted me out of my dream-like state and I realized what I'd been missing. Our youngest pack mate wasn't lying wounded by her cousin's side, and a quick glance up and down the trail showed no signs of her smaller form either. The girl was well and truly gone.

Cinnamon stirred, although he seemed too exhausted to shift and clue us in to what had recently occurred. Still, his twin bond allowed the pair to speak without words. So I wasn't surprised when Ginger's face became even more grim before she passed along the news.

"It was the same wolves from this morning," she said simply. Then, commanding our pack as if I wasn't even present, she ordered, "Spread out and see if you can find Lia's trail. We might still be able to catch them if we run fast enough."

Glen and Quill had remained four-footed while the trouble twin and I examined our fallen comrade, and they now obeyed Ginger immediately, sniffing in a broadening circle around Cinnamon's bloody body. There would be two trails, I knew, one tracing the path by which the attackers had arrived and one pointing to where they'd gone after doing their dirty work. If Lia was alive and walking, it would be easy to hone in on the proper direction. But if not, we'd be forced to guess which trail wended into the past and which into the future.

Sure enough, Glen yipped once, eyes hooded as he picked out a trail, and Quill soon repeated the gesture from the other side of us. The two wolves looked to me for direction, but how was I supposed to know where Lia had been taken?

The pack bond, my wolf whispered, her voice a mere thread of sound within our shared body. She was right, of course. But I'd barely been able to catch the elusive fragment when in lupine form, and I knew my strength had long since faded beyond the ability to don fur once again.

Still, I had to try. I closed my eyes and concentrated as best I could while Cinnamon's labored breathing and the knowledge that Lia was being drawn further and further away from us with every second of delay tore at my attention.

Nothing. It was like staring down into a well at midnight—any sign of the pack bond was well and truly absent.

So I raised my hands in surrender and guessed. "I don't know, Glen," I said quietly. "How about you take the trail you're on and Quill can take the other?"

Beside me, Ginger growled out her frustration even as she fell back down into fur. I could tell from the drag to her steps as she followed after Quill that the trouble twin was just as exhausted as I was. But she loved her cousin and wasn't willing to relinquish any faint hope that the lost girl might yet be found alive.

I loved Lia too, of course. But there was nothing I could do when shifting again was beyond my abilities. So I settled into the only job remaining—nursing Cinnamon back to health.

***

"Lia's gone," Hunter said, stepping out of the woods moments later. His timing was suspicious and I should have grabbed the thick branch lying just within arm's reach, then threatened the uber-alpha until he left my wounded pack mate alone.

But, instead, I found myself springing to my feet and running toward his strength. Hunter was as naked as I was, probably having shifted only moments earlier, and he didn't seem to know what to do with the body slamming up against his own. After an agonizing pause, though, his muscular arms rose to wrap around me.

His hug was tentative at first. But then his embrace tightened as I clung to his shoulder blades, fighting back tears.

"Dead?" I asked with a gulp when I finally felt capable of opening my mouth without keening.

I stumbled as Hunter thrust me back at arm's length. His dark brows lowered menacingly over amber eyes nearly hidden by enlarged pupils. "Dead?" he parroted back. Wolf-like, he shook his head vigorously as if trying to push water out of his ears. "No, of course not," he continued after searching my face for a moment. "The SSS doesn't kill the halfies they take right away. We have time to find her."

I collapsed onto the leaves like a puppet whose strings had been cut. I'd steeled myself against the worst, and, somehow, hearing that Lia was still alive took that strength right out of me.

"That's good news," Hunter said, clearly confused by my actions. "Right?"

His wolf was so rampant now that I was surprised the bloodling was able to spit out human words. But I appreciated the semblance of humanity since it helped me regain my own senses. Feeling like I was a thousand years old, I nonetheless forced myself back to my feet and grabbed Hunter's hand, leading him over to join me on the ground by Cinnamon's side. The trouble twin had dropped into an exhausted slumber a few minutes earlier, and he seemed to rest easier when I stroked his fur. So I resumed my ministrations while gathering my composure back around me.

"Of course it's a good thing," I said at last. Yes, it was wonderful that Lia was presumably still alive. On the other hand, imagining the sixteen year old's terror at being captured and her fate if we were unable to reach her in time made the pack's recent shared pain over her cut foot seem like a bee sting by comparison.

I just need to make sure we find her as quickly as possible, I decided. Which meant figuring out everything Hunter knew about the Shifter Sanitation Society so we could plan a fast and effective strike.

"What are you doing here?" I demanded, changing gears and looking at Hunter with the assessing gaze I should have used in the first place. My previous show of girlish emotions was embarrassing, and I made up for it now by casting a flurry of questions in the uber-alpha's direction. "How did you find me and how did you know to look for Lia?"

Now it was Hunter's turn to avert his eyes, and I didn't miss the evasiveness in his reply. "I spoke to Savannah Abrams' mother this morning," he said finally. "Imagine my surprise to learn that one Fen Young was also on her way to interrogate the worried parent."

Flared nostrils were the only sign of the uber-alpha's annoyance, but a shiver ran down my spine nonetheless. It looked like my wolf was alert enough for Hunter's dominance to affect us, even if she didn't seem keen on joining in the conversation. Just what I needed—a wolf too weak to help out, but just strong enough to get us both killed.

"Yeah, we were headed that way," I mumbled when my companion seemed to require confirmation of Mrs. Abrams' information. I winced, steeling myself to be struck by a blast of icy alpha dominance.

"I thought we'd agreed that you'd head west?" Hunter said through clenched teeth. But the virtual blow I'd been expecting wasn't forthcoming. And despite the danger possibly lurking in the woods around us and the very real threat that Hunter presented to my weak wolf, I couldn't help but laugh from relief.

"*You* agreed we'd head west," I told my companion firmly. "But my pack and I decided that since Lia and I are halfies and have a vested interest in this issue, we might as well check it out and see what's going on."

There was no way to describe the sound that emerged from Hunter's lips other than "growl." Okay, maybe "snarl" would do the trick too. Not a good sign. It looked like his wolf—always awake, but usually in check—was in almost complete control of their shared body now.

Sure enough, the first hints of fur began sprouting from the skin of Hunter's forearms, and I didn't want to wait around and see what would happen next if the uber-alpha's annoyed animal half won out over his thin veneer of humanity. So I did the only thing I could think of...or maybe I should say the one thing I'd kept thinking about over and over ever since Hunter marched into my life.

I reached across Cinnamon's nearly lifeless body to grab the uber-alpha's hair where skull met neck. Then I pulled his mouth down to meet mine.

As before, Hunter was frozen for an instant by my forwardness. But then his lips claimed my own, and I realized that the reality of kissing the uber-alpha was as different from my earlier daydream as the change in my vision when I left wolf form behind. A world that had once seemed a near gray-scale of blue and pale yellow abruptly exploded into a rainbow of passion.

For several long moments, I forgot about wounded and lost pack mates, weak inner wolves, and sadistic secret societies. There was simply no way to focus on the wider world when the uber-alpha in front of me was sucking my consciousness deep into his soul.

Instead, my reality had tunneled down to two simple facts. Hunter was kissing me. And Hunter was my mate.

CHAPTER 14

"Seriously?" Ginger's angry exclamation hit me at the same moment her body slammed into Hunter's side, deftly knocking us apart. She attacked the uber-alpha with fingernails that worked as well as claws, raking red stripes down her opponent's chest before he was able to capture her hands with his own.

"Cinnamon is dying, Lia is missing, and *this* is what you're doing?" Ginger shrieked, wrenching herself around in Hunter's arms so she could face me. "Kissing *him*?"

"Cinnamon's not dying," I answered, red-faced. Yes, Ginger was right—letting my attraction for Hunter sidetrack me from the really important issues at hand had been a bad move. But I couldn't quite figure out why the young woman was so irate.

Intense worry over her twin was the only feasible explanation, so I rushed to set her mind at ease. "He's stopped bleeding and his vitals are steady. Yes, your brother's hurt and he's exhausted, but he's going to be fine."

I glanced at Hunter, asking him without words to release my pack mate from his grasp. The uber-alpha raised one eyebrow, clearly convinced that Ginger would simply transform back into the blazing ball of fury that had pushed apart our lip-lock if she wasn't imprisoned by his iron grip. Still, he obeyed, unhanding the young woman and taking two long steps backwards as if putting space between himself and a rabid skunk recently released from a live trap.

Ginger immediately dropped to her knees beside her brother, her fingers frantically pushing through the matted fur around his lupine throat until she, presumably, found a pulse. I only then realized that Cinnamon's earlier whining had stilled some time ago, meaning that he had, indeed, looked dead when his sister came on the scene. No wonder a single tear dripped down Ginger's cheek before she angrily dashed it away.

With Cinnamon's vitality confirmed, I thought we were out of the figurative woods. But when the trouble twin rose to her feet once again, her ire was aimed directly at me. "So that's your solution? At the first hint of adversity, you're ready to throw away our hard-earned independence and go to *him* for assistance?"

I wrinkled my brow in confusion. Yes, I'd been thinking about asking Hunter for help in finding Lia, but I hadn't actually voiced my thoughts. Leave it to Ginger to assume that an uncontrollable kiss had instead been a calculated ploy to bring a reluctant ally over to our team.

"Calm down," I told my angry pack mate. Then, glancing in the uber-alpha's direction to see how he'd take my reply, I added: "We're not throwing away any of our independence, but Hunter *is* the obvious solution to finding Lia. He's already been on the trail of the SSS for a while now and he's strong...."

To my relief, Hunter nodded as if agreeing to lend his support to our upcoming adventure. Ginger was less complacent, though.

"He's *strong*," the trouble twin spat back. "Is that all that matters to you? *I'm* strong. *You're* strong...or would be if you didn't keep your wolf on such a tight leash. You and I have been doing fine leading our group together and we'll do even better now that you've finally figured out the pack bond. We don't need a *bloodling* to step between us."

Hunter growled and I glanced away from the angry trouble twin in order to meet the uber-alpha's eyes. Had the object of my affections so quickly changed his mind about helping Lia? I didn't think so. But I got the distinct impression that I was missing something obvious, something that both he and Ginger were dancing around with both their gazes and their words.

This whole argument just didn't make any *sense*. Sure, emotions were high ever since Lia went missing, but I couldn't quite understand why everyone was so angry all of a sudden.

"You're going to have to spell it out for her," Hunter said after a moment of intense silence. It had been obvious that the uber-alpha and the trouble twin shared a deep-seated antipathy ever since they first met, so I was surprised now to see the former pointing his words in Ginger's direction. This was the first time Hunter had deigned to give the trouble twin the time of day, and she certainly didn't seem to deserve his regard after flying off the handle. So why was the uber-alpha eying my friend with something that distinctly resembled pity?

Like a cat watching a ping-pong match, I turned my head to see what Ginger would make of a statement that hadn't clued me in at all. Surely the redhead would be as blindsided by Hunter's non sequitur as I was.

But, instead, she just got angrier. The furious blush on her cheeks now rivaled the color of her hair as she ground out: "Seriously? Like she doesn't know how I feel."

The trouble twin's pair of ice-blue eyes bored into mine, the stare a clear lupine challenge. And if I'd had a wolf worth her salt, the two of us would have inevitably come to blows.

But my animal half was sound asleep and my human side saw no reason to fight over what must be a misunderstanding. So I raised both hands in the air in confused surrender.

"I have no clue what you're talking about," I offered finally when both of my companions seemed unwilling to let the issue—whatever it was—drop until I'd chimed in on the matter. "I understand you're not a fan of Hunter and I understand that you're worried about Lia and Cinnamon. So am I. Well, I mean, so am I to the last two points. But I have to admit I *am* a fan of Hunter. He's never done anything other than help us out of tight spots...."

My voice trailed off as I remembered the event that had initiated our original tight spot. Still, I'd worked past my anger at Hunter for thrusting us unceremoniously out of our original pack. He'd thought he had my best interests at heart, and maybe he'd been right.

More recently, the uber-alpha had proven to be a remarkably steadfast companion and a wolf I was happy to have at my back. So, yes, I stood by my initial assessment. I *was* a fan of Hunter.

"Unbelievable," Ginger said after yet another lengthy silence. "You're telling me you haven't been treating me like a partner all this time, letting me lead hunts and brushing up against me."

Brushing up against her? I shook my head, deciding not to touch that part of her statement with a ten-foot pole. "Of course I let you lead hunts," I said as slowly and as calmly as I could. The two of us needed to remember that we were pack mates in a dicey situation and tone this altercation way the hell down. "Your wolf is the strongest one we've got and mine is chicken shit. It would be absurd to try to take that right away from you."

Ginger clenched her jaw and closed her eyes for a second, clearly trying to rejoin me in the land of rationality. But her next words continued to make no sense. "Okay, let's start over. Why do you think we came with you on this ill-fated expedition into outpack territory in the first place?"

I'd asked myself this same question during many wakeless nights as I listened to my new pack mates slumbering all around me, so this time I had a ready answer for the trouble twin's nosy question. "Well, Glen felt obligated, I think," I said, ashamed of myself for letting any of these young shifters be drawn into my outcast status against their will. "He and I have been pack mates for a lot longer than the rest of you. And after a mutual friend died, I think he felt responsible for making sure I didn't get myself killed too."

Ginger rolled one hand in the air to speed me up. She clearly didn't care why Glen had thrown away a safe life at Haven to follow a half-assed halfie into the wilds of outpack territory.

"Lia, I think, came along because she wanted a half-blood role model," I mused. "Plus, with you there, she felt safe. Cinnamon...."

I looked down at the comatose wolf, my throat tightening as I remembered the danger I'd drawn all of these wolves into due to my own weakness. But Ginger's stern gaze demanded an answer, so I continued with my assessment. "Cinnamon came because you came."

"And why did *I* come?" Ginger asked, pausing between each word as if speaking to a five-year-old...or someone in need of a swift kick in the butt. It was easy to guess which of the two options my companion thought best represented me.

"You came to have fun?" I guessed.

"And is that why you kissed me?" she demanded. "To have fun?"

I wrinkled up my brow in continued confusion and Hunter's growl grew louder and more ominous as Ginger's words rang out across the still forest air. "I didn't kiss you," I replied, my words finally taking on a bite of their own. I knew I called Ginger a trouble twin, but I hadn't expected the young woman to take her name quite so literally while we were in such a precarious situation. "You kissed *me* to get Quill's attention."

Now it was Ginger's turn to growl. And, to my surprise, Hunter broke out into a laugh in response. "Completely clueless, remember?" he rumbled from the other side of me.

The young woman who ably held all of our attention in her manicured hands took a deep breath, and for a split second I thought I could feel her heightened emotions within my own belly. That rabid skunk I mentioned earlier? It seemed to be tearing my friend apart from the inside out.

I winced, hoping Ginger would hurry up and put us both out of our misery. But when she spoke, I had to admit I'd rather have maintained my previous blissful ignorance.

"I joined your pack, I led your hunts, I *kissed you*, because I loved you," the young woman muttered.

And even through my shock, I couldn't miss her pointed use of the past tense.

***

"I..." I started to say I was sorry to have led Ginger on. But I hadn't led her on, at least not purposefully. I'd just assumed she enjoyed filling her position of power within our pack. I'd merely treated her like a girl friend.

A friend who's a girl, that is. Not a *girl*friend.

Ack! I was beginning to see why Ginger might have been confused by the whole situation.

"But you're always flirting with guys," I said finally, trying to understand. "That whole bar full of outpack males last night. Quill. Everyone."

"I was just trying to get your attention," the teenager muttered, eyes averted.

Abruptly, I felt sorry for her. Ginger was a pack princess and had almost certainly been cosseted her entire life. While I only had two additional years on her, my halfie heritage and the months I'd spent clanless during my time as a troubled teenager had forced me to grow up fast. As a result, I couldn't remember ever feeling as young as Ginger currently appeared.

So I apologized after all. "I'm sorry," I said, reaching out to pull her into a hug, then changing my mind at the last minute and instead merely patting her shoulder. "It's no reflection on you that I'm not interested, though. I just don't swing that way."

"You don't *swing* that way?" Ginger flicked one painted nail through my untended hair, trailed the same fingertip down across my tattooed arms. "This and this and your so-called *wardrobe*, and you're telling me you're *straight?*"

I shrugged, hoping against hope that the trouble twin would laugh at my unintentional misrepresentation of my sexuality and let the whole misunderstanding slide. Yes, she'd lost face by hankering after someone who wasn't available, but I'd lost face with my rough dress. So we were even, right?

Wrong.

"Not that it matters now," Ginger said, taking a firm step away from me and picking up a shiny, metallic object that she must have dropped at our feet when attacking Hunter. "The real issue is that you don't have the foggiest clue how to be an alpha. You trust this...this...." She shook her head furiously, clearly unable to come up with a slur strong enough to describe how she felt about the uber-alpha in front of her.

"Asshole?" Hunter suggested unhelpfully.

"Oh, thanks so much for pointing out how you self-identify," Ginger said, verbally tearing into him for thinking he could complete her sentence.

But Hunter's chosen moniker was only a side note in the scathing tear-down the trouble twin had in store for me. Thrusting the object into my hand, she demanded. "*Look* at this."

Obediently, I turned the shiny thing over and over in my fingers, trying to understand what I was seeing. It resembled a twisted razor blade, but one that was sharp on all sides rather than on just a single surface. I nicked my finger merely examining it, and I wished one of us had been wearing clothes so we could put the treacherous object safely into a pocket before someone else got hurt.

Still, I had no idea what I was looking at. So I raised my eyebrows at the trouble twin in question once again.

She flared her nostrils, clearly thinking no explanation should have been necessary. And, as she elaborated, I figured she was right—a real shifter would have understood the metallic object's past use immediately. Because a real shifter would have been able to smell Lia's blood clinging to its sharp edges.

"I found this razor on the path where Lia cut her foot," Ginger explained, spelling it out for me since I was clearly too slow to make the necessary connections on my own. "Someone dropped it there specifically to injure her so she'd end up separated from the pack and easy to kidnap. Someone who's been sniffing around our group for weeks on end, looking for a weak link. Someone," she added, pointing a finger at Hunter, "exactly like him."

CHAPTER 15

The uber-alpha was lupine in an instant. The hairs on his ruff came menacingly erect and he advanced in absolute silence toward the female trouble twin. Hunter had passed the point of warning, I saw, and was now prepared to deal with the female who had been a thorn in his paw ever since their first introduction.

True to her nickname, Ginger was also ready and willing to meet her opponent on the field of battle. But she'd shifted one too many times that day already and her clenched teeth and strained features made no difference against the simple physics of exhaustion. Instead, she remained clad in thin human skin, no fur and wolf hide forthcoming to protect her from the other shifter's imminent attack.

I guess that means saving my unruly pack mate's neck is up to me.

"*Stop!*" I ordered, flinging myself between the two combatants. I didn't expect my command to do any good against the uber-alpha...especially since Ginger had made a very valid point about his sudden presence at the exact same moment Lia had gone missing. Rationally, I knew that I should be joining the trouble twin in driving the danger out of our clan.

But, irrationally, I trusted Hunter. He wouldn't have hurt Cinnamon. He wouldn't have kidnapped Lia. And, now, he wouldn't tear through me to get to my obstreperous pack mate.

Or so I hoped. Despite my best intentions to stand as tall and brave as Ginger behind me, my whole body quaked when it dawned on me that Hunter's sharp teeth had ended up inches away from my bare thigh.

The wolf raised one side of his lip in what might have been a snarl...but was, I soon realized, instead the lupine equivalent of a leer. Yes, I *had* just thrown my crotch directly up against my opponent's nose. All he'd have to do was open his mouth to lick the portion of my anatomy that was feeling distinctly moist....

"This...this...." I lost all grasp of nouns for a moment, but pushed forward nonetheless. "This whatever-it-is can be dealt with later," I said firmly, alternating glances between the irate trouble twin and the amused uber-alpha. "Right now, we need to get Cinnamon some medical attention and then figure out how we're going to find Lia. So the two of you can just get over yourselves for the moment. That's final."

Fake it 'til you make it. My favorite technique, remarkably, seemed to work just as well on a wolf-brain uber-alpha and an incensed pack mate as it did on the world at large. Because Hunter promptly sank into a lupine sit and reached jaws over one shoulder to tease a burr out of his matted fur. Meanwhile, Ginger released the clenched fists that had been resting on her ample hips and crouched back down by her brother's side. Cat-like, the pair of antagonists was momentarily united in the belief that the best course of action was to pretend they'd never menaced each other in the first place.

Disaster averted.

Or *mostly* averted. "This isn't over, backstabber," the trouble twin muttered just low enough that I could pretend not to hear.

I tensed, waiting for Hunter to dive back into the field of battle. But his ears merely flicked forward briefly then away, accepting the verbal sally without comment.

Before Ginger could prick at the uber-alpha's pride further, Glen and Quill came bounding out of the woods together. To my supreme relief, the scene greeting them looked remarkably like a group of three worried pack mates rather than like enemy armies preparing for battle. And when Glen glanced a quick question at me, I nodded permission for my beta to shift into human form and hoist Cinnamon over one broad shoulder.

"Let's go," I ordered before Hunter or Ginger could renew aggressions. And we turned as a unit—albeit a very disjointed one—to head back toward the parking area that we'd left so gleefully behind only an hour earlier.

***

"This is a wolf, not a dog," the vet said as soon as he walked into the crowded examining room to find a comatose Cinnamon lying atop his examining table.

"Part wolf," I lied glibly, repeating the commonly used pretense that our animal forms were just big puppy dogs and no danger to the general public. "He's harmless, I promise. Gentle as a lamb."

"Uh huh," Dr. Anderson answered, disbelief evident in his voice. He rolled up both sleeves to display a network of scars running up his forearms. "This and this and this were caused by harmless animals too. And *this* one," he pointed to yet another pale line welting his skin, "was made by an actual lamb."

My pack and I stopped breathing as one. Yes, we *could* get back on the road and keep driving until we found a second clinic. But Cinnamon hadn't so much as opened his eyes since we'd carefully placed him in the car in the first place. Despite our best efforts to stem the flow of blood, our wounded companion was still leaking vital fluids, and every moment we spent seeking assistance felt like a year hacked off the trouble twin's life expectancy.

I opened my mouth to plead with the human, but he sighed and caved before I could do so. "I'll treat him, but he needs to be muzzled and restrained," Dr. Anderson said firmly.

Around me, three male shifters and I all released sighs of relief. But Ginger was less impressed. Instead, the sound emanating from her throat was a full-formed lupine growl, proof of a loss of control she had never before exhibited around non-shifterkind.

Before I could sidetrack her, the female pushed forward into the vet's face. I held my breath, hoping she'd fall back on her usual weapon of heightened sex appeal in order to solve this problem. But the young woman neither pushed out her breasts nor ran a hand across her full lips. Instead, worry over her brother's waning health had worn away any semblance of civility.

"He's not even *conscious*," the trouble twin said, her words just short of a shriek and her face more reminiscent of a harpy than a Barbie. Ginger pushed both hands hard against Dr. Anderson's lab-coated chest and knocked him back a step with the force of her blow. "He's losing blood as we speak. He needs *help*. Just stitch him up. *Please*."

I was pretty sure that last word had never before come out of my friend's mouth. But the vet wasn't swayed. "Look, *ma'am*," he said, clearly rethinking his willingness to deal with the crazy people who came along with the wild wolf. "Restraints won't hurt him. They'll just protect us all from an animal who's clearly a scrapper."

As if to illustrate his point, Dr. Anderson motioned at the wounds that covered Cinnamon's unmoving body. And I had to admit the doctor had a good point. In the animal world, a beast who kept fighting while his hide was being torn to shreds wasn't the kind of patient any vet would want on his operating table. In fact, we were probably lucky Dr. Anderson hadn't turned us out of his clinic already.

Little did the man in front of us know that Cinnamon was the most laid-back member of our little band of werewolves. Both his human and his animal natures were inherently gentle 99% of the time. The twin's mean streak only came out when he was trying to protect a cousin who was more like a kid sister than a distant relation.

A cousin who was probably being driven further and further away from our current location with each moment that we wasted discussing muzzles. Muzzles that Cinnamon wouldn't care less about even if he were awake.

"Okay," I agreed for the lot of us, grabbing Ginger's arm and pulling her out of the vet's line of sight. Without looking behind me, I gave the redhead a push away from the conversation, and I felt more than saw that Glen immediately pulled the unhappy female into the confinement of a hug. As usual, my second was ready to deal with every problem I threw his way, both literally and figuratively.

"We'll put any restraints on him that you want," I added. *Just hurry*, I finished silently.

I could have sworn that Dr. Anderson read the unspoken words in my eyes, which I guess wasn't so surprising since he was trained to deal with animals who couldn't speak in words. Whatever the reason, the vet nodded and left through a back door rather than launching into the lecture I was pretty sure we had coming about the dangers of keeping even a half-wolf on a leash.

I'd heard it all before. *Canis lupus* is inherently unpredictable, the vet would tell us. A wolf isn't a dog, willing to do what you tell him to while looking up at you with soulful eyes and begging for a treat. No, a wolf is always striving for increased power, watching and waiting for the moment he can tear you down and take his rightful place as the leader of your pack.

Despite myself, I met Hunter's eyes across my friends' heads and shivered. The vet's lecture—or the one I imagined Dr. Anderson wanted to make—resonated far too well with our current situation. I hadn't been lying when I said Cinnamon was as gentle as a lamb, but maybe Ginger had been right about the wolf who I'd recently allowed to wiggle into both my pack and my heart.

But, with only moments to spare before the vet returned, I shook the notion out of my mind and instead got the group moving once again. "We don't all need to be crowded around here while Dr. Anderson stitches Cinnamon up. Glen, maybe you could call Mrs. Abrams and let her know we won't be coming today after all? Quill, could you make a spot in your van where Cinnamon will be more comfortable once the vet's done?"

I cringed as I thought of the way we'd tossed the wounded wolf into the back of our car atop that already bloodstained tent fly during our most recent journey. The repeated visual—first a dead SSS member then a nearly dead pack mate—didn't escape me. Whether or not Cinnamon would indeed be more comfortable in Quill's van, I'd definitely feel less guilt-stricken about the arrangement.

"Sure," Glen agreed, and Quill also offered an easy nod as the two males walked out together.

"Ginger," I began, trying to think of a task I could set for the trouble twin in order to get her out of our hair while Dr. Anderson operated on her brother. I figured she'd be better off not seeing the extent of Cinnamon's injuries with fur shaved away, and she clearly had issues with the concept of her twin constrained by a muzzle.

But before I could dream up a suitable assignment, Ginger had turned her anger back in my direction. "I'll stay right here," she said. "I'm not leaving Cinnamon's side while that *traitor* is present. I can't believe you even let him come in here with us in the first place."

In my defense, I hadn't actually *let* Hunter go anywhere. When we'd returned to the small gravel parking lot, we found a shiny new SUV sitting between Quill's faded VW bus and our old, dented jalopy. Hunter had deftly removed the unfamiliar vehicle's key from a magnetic hideaway beneath the wheel well, then he'd donned a slick suit that made him look like an entirely different person from the bloodling I'd recently gotten to know.

From the beginning, I'd understood that Hunter was the primary enforcer for the regional shifter Tribunal. But seeing his fancy wheels and the strong semblance of humanity he now wore like a second skin put his presence in an entirely different perspective. It was more than obvious that I had neither the right nor the ability to prevent the uber-alpha from tagging along on our journey.

Not that I'd tried very hard to send him away. Okay, I hadn't tried at all. Instead, it had soothed my pinched gut to glance in the rear-view mirror and find that Hunter's SUV remained part of our entourage during the hour-long journey to the nearest veterinary clinic.

Of course, that explanation would definitely set the trouble twin off. So I decided to deal with the elephant in the room instead. "Hunter, maybe you could tell Ginger how you were able to find us this afternoon?" I prodded. Honestly, I wanted to know the answer to this question myself, the uber-alpha's previous evasion of the issue having niggled at the back of my mind ever since Ginger threw the challenge up in his face back in the woods.

Despite the fact that his wolf was probably lying in wait just beneath the surface, Hunter now looked like an after-hours businessman with his white shirt unbuttoned just far enough to show a little chest hair. And his response to my question was urbane enough to match his new appearance. "Is that something you really want me to share?" he asked smoothly. One eyebrow raised as he directed the question at the trouble twin instead of at me.

Ginger glared back at him, her own efforts at humanity becoming more lackluster by the moment. In fact, I was pretty sure the female's canines were longer than usual when she opened her mouth to reply. "Why wouldn't I want to know?" she demanded. "It's pretty fishy, don't you think? You buttering up my naive little cousin, then Lia suddenly going missing mere minutes before you show back up in our lives. Are you trying to say that's all just a coincidence?"

Before Hunter could answer, a thin whine brought all of our attention back around to the wounded wolf lying atop the cold steel examining table. As one, we allowed the argument to drop as we clustered in a little circle surrounding Cinnamon. My relief at finding him awake and alert actually made me a little weak in the knees.

"You're going to be okay, you big lug," Ginger said soothingly, stroking her brother's ears gently and pretending not to notice the blood rubbing off from his fur onto her fingertips. Her previous show of lupine aggression had disappeared as quickly as it came, her body language now both calm and calming. "You've just gotta be brave and put on some BDSM ware for the sake of the good doctor," she added, managing to sound wry instead of annoyed.

I could have sworn Cinnamon grinned despite the intense pain he must have been experiencing. But the battered wolf shook his head as if to push the focus of our conversation away from his lacerations. Then he stretched his neck over so he could stick his nose into Ginger's pocket.

"I don't have anything good in there," his sister replied, but she dutifully disinterred the contents anyway. "I know you missed lunch, which has got to be *way* more traumatic than any mauling," she continued to patter as a couple of napkins with scrawled phone numbers, a tube of lipstick, and finally her cell phone came tumbling out to land on the metal surface beside Cinnamon's wet nose. "But once you're all stitched up, Fen will buy you the juiciest hamburger you've ever seen. Or maybe a steak. How about that?"

In a completely uncharacteristic display of fixation, Cinnamon showed no interest in the delights on his culinary agenda. Instead, he struggled to his feet, pulling open partially scabbed-over wounds in the process so blood once again started dropping splat by splat onto the now smeared operating table.

"Hey, shh," Ginger said, trying to push her brother back down. "You need to stay calm for just a few more minutes...."

Submissive Cinnamon generally did whatever his sister said. But now he ignored Ginger's admonitions and poked at her cell phone with his nose. Despite lacking thumbs, he managed to swipe the device to life—and leave a smear of wolf boogers on the screen in the process—before the phone tumbled off the edge of the table and clattered to the tile floor.

Ginger's attachment to her cell phone was a subject of frequent teasing in our little pack. Still, the look on the trouble twin's face as she peered down at the screen went above and beyond any obsession with possibly damaged electronics. "Oh no," she whispered, one hand covering her mouth.

"Oh yes," Hunter said grimly, picking up the cell phone and handing it to me so I could see what had gotten everyone so riled up.

For a moment, I was confused. I barely used my own phone except for planning out driving routes and stopping points. So it took me a moment to realize what I was seeing.

There was Ginger's Facebook page, five thousand friends proving that she was as popular in the electronic world as she'd been on top of that bar table last night. There was her profile icon, in which she appeared to be wearing nothing at all except a smile.

And there was her most recent status update, telling precisely when and where we'd decided to hunt for our lunch.

CHAPTER 16

The realization that *she* had been the one setting the SSS on our heels all this time shut Ginger up long enough for Dr. Anderson to repair her brother and send us on our way with one bottle of antibiotics and another of painkillers. "With any other patient, I'd offer to keep him overnight," the vet said quietly as Ginger fluttered around her twin and Hunter scooped the wounded werewolf up off the operating table as easily as if the hundred-plus-pound animal was a grocery bag full of toilet paper. "But I really don't want to risk a wounded wolf waking up around people he doesn't know."

The man's eyes bored into mine, and the lecture I knew was coming created a near-solid wall in the air between us. I sighed and caved.

"You're going to give me the phone number of a wolf-rescue agency now," I said, providing the human with the opening he needed to rebuild his own peace of mind. It was the least I could do when Dr. Anderson had been so kind despite being less than thrilled to have a supposedly wild animal on his operating table. The vet had been a consummate professional regardless of his reservations, his hands gentle on Cinnamon's lacerated skin. He deserved this opportunity to vent his feelings.

"No. Well yes, but...." Dr. Anderson closed his eyes for a moment, and I could tell he was wavering between speaking his mind or just letting us go.

And as much as I wanted to get out the door before Ginger lost control of her inner animal or Cinnamon accidentally went two-legged, I paused. My sleepy wolf was nudging me wordlessly, as if she'd noticed something about our preceding exchange that I'd missed. And since my animal half seemed unwilling or unable to clue me in further, I figured I'd better get the doctor's feedback after all.

So I used everything I'd learned about body language to put the veterinarian more at ease. I rounded my shoulders, dipped my chin down, and opened my mouth in unstated question. It seemed like a lot of effort just to bring on the same spiel I'd heard a dozen times before. But if the gesture would make my inner wolf happy....

And Dr. Anderson took the bait. "I know this sounds unbelievable since large predators were eradicated from this area centuries ago," he said quietly. "But I'm certain I've seen a pack of gray wolves around here multiple times over the last few weeks. Not coyotes, but *wolves*. So, if you don't want Cinnamon getting torn up a second time, it's probably safer to keep your pet indoors for a while."

The human rubbed one hand across his close-cropped beard as if second-guessing his assessment even as he made it. But I held no doubts on that score. From what little Hunter had told me, the SSS had thoroughly claimed this portion of outpack territory as their own. It wouldn't surprise me at all if the same rogue shifters ignored the rules against being seen by humans and simply ran when and where they wanted to as a pack.

"Any place in particular?" I asked carefully, trying not to put my growing excitement on display. This might be the clue we needed to discover where Lia and Savannah Abrams were being held, and it was all I could do not to grab onto the veterinarian's shoulders and shake the information right out of him.

"Multiple locations," Dr. Anderson answered, confusion evident on his face. I obviously hadn't produced the reaction he was expecting, and I kicked myself for not throwing a little shock and worry into the mix before diving directly into question time. Oh well, what was done was done, and it looked like I'd gotten all the information I was going to get.

I opened my mouth to thank the vet. But before I could speak, Dr. Anderson dredged up a little more data.

"The one place I've heard about them the most is out on state route 603, down past the county landfill. A couple of farmers who live in that direction said a wolf pack shows up like clockwork every Friday evening around dusk." The vet smiled, amused by the idea that wild animals planned out their lives by clock and calendar. "I'd be willing to bet that any howls are just high-school kids having a good time, though," he added. "There aren't many unattended places to go around here if you're underage and want to yuk it up."

Dr. Anderson shrugged, and I let the subject drop, thanking him profusely for his time and for the care he'd taken with Cinnamon. But, inside, I was dancing with glee.

Because, Hunter had told us that the SSS didn't kill their prey right away, that they instead seemed to save the captured half-wolves to be murdered ceremoniously. And what better place to disembowel a young female than down a deserted country road where even wolf sightings barely caused the neighbors to raise an eyebrow?

***

131

We had forty-eight hours until Lia would be frog-marched across a secluded pasture, tied down, and used to fill some void within the SSS's darkened souls. Forty-eight hours to make a plan, to do enough legwork to ensure said plan wouldn't result in our youngest pack mate's demise, and to rebuild the inter-shifter connections that I was certain would be critical to our strategy's eventual success.

So what did we do first? Take a long nap, of course.

It seemed that Hunter's role as Tribunal enforcer had some perks after all, the most evident of which was a credit card with no apparent limit. I could almost see the word *Suh-weet!* appear in a thought bubble above Cinnamon's lupine head when our not-quite-pack-mate showed us the entire floor of a nearby Holiday Inn that he'd rented out for our use. Then, after a couple of hours of shut-eye, a delivery guy dropped off what appeared to be enough food to fuel a moderate-sized army, and even Ginger started looking at the uber-alpha with a bit more fondness in her eyes.

We ate with the wild abandon of wolves, our animal halves understanding that warm calories would go a long way toward easing the ache that had taken up residence in the pits of our stomachs. The meat and carbs were gone in a heartbeat and our paper plates were bare save a few stray florets of broccoli when I finally I broke the silence. "We need to make a plan," I told the shifters spread out across the giant king-sized bed, chairs, and floor in the room we'd gravitated toward. What can I say—you can lead a crowd of werewolves to separate rooms, but you can't make the pack sleep apart.

"A plan sounds good," Ginger agreed, but her tone wasn't as agreeable as it might have been. I'd hoped that a couple of hours of sleep followed by the vision of her brother limping around on his own four paws would set the young woman's mind at ease. But, instead, she remained just as prickly as she'd been ever since stumbling upon Hunter's and my first kiss.

"Problem?" I asked, figuring we might as well get that bee out of her bonnet. Ginger didn't so much smolder as seethe. And the longer you let her stew, the hotter the flames of her anger became when they eventually erupted out into the open.

"Yes, since you ask, there *is* a problem," Ginger agreed. She gave Hunter the evil eye and proceeded to beat the dead horse that we'd already pounded about half a mile into the earth. "Our plan should be shared with *pack mates only*. And *he's* not pack."

I closed my eyes and took a deep breath before speaking to make sure my own words didn't come out sounding equally bitter. "We've been over this already, Ginger. Hunter may not be part of this pack, but he cares about Lia. And, in case you haven't figured it out yet, it's his *job* to track down the SSS. That's why he can afford to put us up here." I waved my hands around at the spic-and-span furnishings that put our previous night's accommodations to shame.

"Oh, and now your head is turned by *money?*" the trouble twin demanded.

The issue was a ludicrous waste of time, especially after Ginger had proven to all of our satisfaction that she, rather than Hunter, had been the unwitting traitor in our midst. Luckily, there was one easy way to shut her up.

"Okay, we'll vote on it," I caved, knowing that everyone else had a more rational understanding of our need for the uber-alpha's support during the hunt ahead. Surely our other pack mates understood that there was no reason to dive into a rescue with only butter knives when we could take a machine gun to the fight.

To my surprise, the pack bond flickered to life in the air before me as I spoke, and I slid my gaze around the room to see if anyone else had noticed the strange phenomenon. Nope, no dropped jaws and expressions of surprise. No inventive swear words and half-baked theories. So the glowing lines that now bounced back and forth between us as if alive were only there for me to see...assuming I wasn't hallucinating the image.

To test that hypothesis, I tugged gently on the strand connecting me with Glen. And to my surprise, my second spoke up as if I'd nudged him physically. "Yes, definitely. We need every shifter we can get our hands on to protect Lia. Hunter is an asset."

I nodded with approval and reached forward next to tweak the tether connecting me to Ginger. This strand of starlight was twice as wide as the others, as if the energy the trouble twin had invested in her misplaced crush had built up our connection beyond ordinary levels. *I hope that means she'll start to see reason soon*, I thought as I plucked the glowing thread like a guitar string.

"Ow!" Ginger flinched back as if I'd struck her and I raised my hands skyward in apology. *Sorry*, I mouthed. I guess I hadn't realized the full power of the pack bond after all.

To remedy my faux pas, I visualized sending a ball of calming energy down the line. And to my surprise the effort bore immediate fruit. Ginger's tense posture relaxed a trifle and she graced me with her signature one-sided smile, the one which had been distinctly lacking during the previous twelve hours.

Still, when the trouble twin spoke, she hadn't changed her tune. "No," she said simply.

That was exactly what I'd expected, so I didn't argue the point and instead turned my attention to Cinnamon. The wounded wolf had collapsed onto the bed beside his sister after stuffing his face with pizza and sweet-and-sour chicken, and he barely raised his muzzle out of his sister's lap when the attention of the pack turned in his direction. Poor guy was probably having trouble tracking our conversation despite his recent nap, and I hoped we could send him back to bed in short order.

Still, Cinnamon was apparently following along well enough to know I was waiting for his decision on Hunter's tenure within our band. *No.* The word materialized within my mind, and now it was my turn to jolt in surprise at the mixture of emotions that traveled along with the word down our shared tether. The pack bond's depth of connection continued to astound me.

I opened my mouth to translate for those still in the dark. But the male trouble twin was way ahead of me, shaking his head in a visual confirmation of his predictable stance. Cinnamon might have been bosom buddies with Hunter in any other situation, but he would now and forever choose to back his sister up. So he, like Ginger, voted to have the uber-alpha summarily ejected from our pack.

I shrugged and motioned to Quill. The cowboy shifter would vote yes, then I'd break the tie, I knew. Ginger would inevitably grouse and moan for a few hours. But we'd eventually get where we needed to go—toward a newfound pack solidarity that allowed us to rely on Hunter's uber-alpha abilities when needed. Our pack would no longer be divided, and our shared skills would make short work of busting Lia out of her prison.

Or not. "No, I don't trust him," Quill said quietly. His tether to the group was barely visible, a tiny thread that hardly reached beyond the closest pack mate—Ginger. Even my own connection to the cowboy shifter was invisible across the ten-foot distance that lay between us, and I couldn't feel his presence in my mind at all.

In contrast, I noticed now that Hunter's tie to our pack was much more obvious than the other male's. Actually, the brilliance and width of the uber-alpha's intangible bond was twice as thick as the one connecting me to Ginger, meaning that it was also considerably stronger than the iron tether that bound the two twins together.

Okay, so that wasn't entirely true. Yes, Hunter was linked into our group more firmly than anyone else was. But his linkage wasn't really to the pack as a whole. It was to me alone.

Not quite right, my wolf reiterated, our shared slumber having given her the energy to kibitz at will. *The bond....*

Later, I ordered. I didn't care if Ginger and Cinnamon and Quill...and even my animal half...didn't trust the uber-alpha. Hunter was bound to me —I could see that with my own two eyes. And the tether we shared was enough to prove that he had our best interests at heart.

So I dismantled the previously democratic governance of our pack with a single sentence. "I appreciate everyone's feedback," I stated firmly, "but Hunter is in."

And, in front of my eyes, the tether that had bound me to Ginger snapped in half, my weaker tie to Cinnamon disappearing right along with his sister's. My eyes widened as the broken ropes of light flung back in my direction, the recoil knocking me backwards against the wall as the bitter ends hit.

I lay there stunned for a solid minute. And when I finally shook off the pain and opened my eyes, no indication of our previous clan cohesion was now visible in the air.

I wanted to think the pack bond's current absence was simply in my own mind, a reaction to having been literally slapped in the face by Ginger's dismay. Surely this was just another example of the recoil I'd experienced earlier that afternoon when I fumbled the network of threads and dropped the cat's cradle of connection into a tangled mass at my feet.

Yes, that former incident had been painful for both me and my wolf, but we'd been able to pick the pack bond back up after a nice long nap then. I hoped we'd be equally capable of resurrecting the clan connections this time around as well.

But I had a bad feeling that what I'd just witnessed was instead the dismantling of a troupe that had never been fully bonded to their alpha in the first place. And the vastly increased pain in my gut suggested that we'd just lost the one ace in the hole we possessed in our upcoming battle against the Shifter Sanitation Society.

CHAPTER 17

"Today we plan and practice," the uber-alpha said the next morning. "Tomorrow we rest. Then we hit the ground running thirty-six hours from now at sunset. So let's make those minutes count."

Every gaze in the room turned to meet mine, waiting to see how I'd react to the fact that Hunter had effectively wrested control of our current operation out of my grip. I didn't see what the big deal was, though. It wasn't as if I'd ever been the kind of alpha who refused to share leadership opportunities. Case in point—the fact that Ginger and Glen had been heading up our fur-form hunts for as long as we'd been together.

Still, I *did* have some agenda items to add to Hunter's simplistic analysis of the situation. "Sounds good," I agreed, then began tossing out orders. "Ginger, I want you to see if you can find any evidence of the SSS online. They've got to be communicating somehow, and the internet is the most effective way to do that. Secret Facebook groups, members-only forums, email lists. See what you can dig up."

"No need to teach your grandmother how to suck eggs," the trouble twin muttered. Her eyes were still flashing from her earlier annoyance, but she obediently pulled out her smartphone and got to work. As our most internet savvy pack member, I trusted that if any evidence was out there on the World Wide Web, Ginger would find it.

"Glen, we need some sort of tracking device. Small, easy to hide against the skin, and with a long range."

"On it," my second agreed, but his eyes were troubled. I could tell he'd already made the mental leap and knew where I was going with this request. But all he said was, "Okay if I take the car?"

"All yours," I said, tossing over the keys from the top of the bureau beside me.

Then I turned my gaze to the Tribunal enforcer, whose eyes were narrowing with suspicion. "Hunter, do you think you can scout out the meeting grounds, see if you catch any sign of shifters without leaving your own scent trail behind? It would be nice to know if we have the right location now rather than showing up at an empty field tomorrow evening."

I'd hoped the challenge would be enough to derail him from putting two and two together and figuring out what I intended to do the next day. Because even though Hunter hadn't repeated his four-letter assessment of our relationship—or our kiss—I had a feeling the uber-alpha wouldn't be thrilled by my plan B.

No such luck. "Quill can do that," Hunter growled, his stare boring into my face so strongly that I found myself incapable of looking away.

My wolf must have been more alert than usual after nine hours prone on an actual mattress, because I felt the uber-alpha's emotions as if they were a physical substance creeping up my legs and invading my skin. Everything around me became muffled, a ringing started up within my ears, and I couldn't so much as swallow down the lump that had lodged within my throat.

To my surprise, support emerged from an unlikely location. My wolf—weak, lily-livered coward that she usually was—came to my aid. She rose up through our shared body, pushing my human consciousness out of the way and peering out from behind our eyes. Then, with a show of force that had nothing to back it up, she snarled and snapped at the uber-alpha. And to my surprise, the fog stifling my senses abruptly receded.

Hunter glanced aside for an instant as if chagrined by his own over-reaction. But when he turned back in my direction, he wasn't ready to let the issue drop. "If you plan to use yourself as bait," he said, the words an order, "then it's high time you learned how to handle that hunk of metal you carry around. Turn it into a real weapon rather than a walking stick. Let's go."

***

"I'm not going to swing at you," I said to the werewolf who currently glared at me from the other side of the clearing.

An hour ago, Hunter had dragged me away from my pack and into the air-conditioned comfort of his SUV. He'd deftly wound up curvy, gravel roads into the national forest until we reached a secluded pull-off spot not much different from the one where we'd begun our ill-fated hunt the day before. Then, wordlessly, he led me to the location where I now stood contemplating the idea of hacking into someone who I was tentatively beginning to call a friend, cutting him apart with a katana so sharp it could slice smooth lines through thick paper. The training exercise seemed like a very bad idea.

"I've been watching you," the uber-alpha said quietly, circling around me with such soft footfalls that I barely believed he still retained his human form. The wolf that was always rampant behind his eyes now seemed to be speaking through the human's lips, and I shivered at the force of his words.

"You use that sword so you don't have to call upon your animal half," my companion continued. "That I understand—when she sleeps, you're protected from alpha compulsions. It's smart to work to your strengths."

I wouldn't precisely call my half-assed wolf a strength, but Hunter appeared to be trying to give me a compliment. So I nodded cagily, waiting for the other shoe to drop.

It didn't take long for him to get to the point. "But you just defend, defend, defend," the uber-alpha continued smoothly as he stalked around in a circle, making me swivel to face him. "That's not going to be enough to spring Lia from the SSS."

I shook my head, not in negation of my companion's analysis but in an effort to push aside the obvious facts. Yes, Hunter was right. If it came down to choosing Lia's safety over that of a nameless psycho shifter, the answer was obvious. I would skewer those suckers.

Still, that didn't mean I was willing to hack Hunter apart until he looked like Cinnamon just for the sake of practice. In fact, the thought accelerated my heart rate even more as it drew to mind the wounded trouble twin's actions this very morning.

Cinnamon had been bound and determined to help with today's preparations. But he'd barely managed to shift into human form and state his willingness to join our strike force before conking back out on the bed. In response, I'd met Ginger's eyes and she'd nodded her understanding. On that one point we were in full agreement—Cinnamon would not be a part of the action tomorrow even if we had to chain him to a table leg to achieve that end.

"Focus," the uber-alpha said softly.

Blinking my eyes to clear my mind, I realized my opponent had taken advantage of my wandering thoughts to step so close he could have reached out and pulled the sword out of my clenched fists. Which is precisely what I thought he planned to do at first, until I realized the uber-alpha was instead slipping a thin skin over the length of my blade. The motion was so reminiscent of rolling on a condom that I flushed beet red.

Nice visual, my wolf whispered. Beside me, Hunter's lips quirked up in response, and I almost thought he'd caught the gist of the animal's words.

Shh, I growled more than whispered. Then, aloud, I demanded to know: "What's that?"

"Protection," Hunter answered, laughter rippling beneath his simple answer. The evocative pun begged the question—could my companion really have read my mind?

I shook my head to dislodge what I knew to be an impossibility. Unless I put effort into sending communications from myself to another pack mate, I'd never heard another shifter's words inside my head and I doubted my companions had ever heard mine. We were werewolves, not mind readers.

"You'd still end up bruised as anything even if I can't cut into you," I said, turning aside the dangerous direction of our nonverbal conversation by dint of focusing on our equally dangerous physical reality.

"But I won't be bloody," Hunter amended. "It won't be the first or the last time I've been knocked around, and bruises won't impact my ability to fight tomorrow." Then the air shimmered ever so slightly as he twisted to one side, managing to drop his clothes emptily to the ground as he achieved sleek lupine stature more quickly than any shifter I'd ever met before.

Hunter was beautiful as a wolf. Beautiful like a shiny torpedo or an approaching tornado, that is. He growled and lunged forward as if to strike, and despite myself I flung my sword up between us in guard position.

The uber-alpha wasn't on the defensive at all, and I could have easily thrust my weapon deep into his belly, jerked down, and ended the battle then and there. Well, I could have if my katana hadn't sported a padded tip that would prevent it from piercing an apple, let alone a wolf's tough hide.

There wasn't time to think, though. Battle was all about adrenaline and instinct, so I did what I'd done dozens of times before. I smacked Hunter hard on the shoulder with the flat of my blade, knocking him back a step but leaving no permanent damage in the blow's wake.

In response, I could have sworn the words *Not good enough* floated up in my mind, their timbre flavored with Hunter's deep rumble rather than with my own higher-pitched tones. I shook the thought away though because the uber-alpha was already lunging forward again, this time so quickly that he slipped beneath my guard and wrapped his jaws around my ankle with the strength of a steel trap.

I expected my companion to soften his bite just as I'd eased off on my own cut. But, instead, the bloodling clenched down until I could feel his sharp canines shredding my jeans and then piercing the skin underneath. I jerked back in surprise, feeling blood welling up to wet my sock.

"You bit me?" I couldn't decide whether I was shocked or horrified. We weren't *that* kind of werewolf. Sure, if danger faced our pack mates, then we were willing to defend our friends and ourselves. But we didn't go around chomping down on humans or on other shifters just for the fun of it.

The image of Daisy Rambler rose up in my mind unbidden. The shifters who had turned her young body into a piece of meat more suited to a slaughterhouse than to a morgue hadn't felt any compunction about biting into a living shifter. They wouldn't hesitate to do the same for Savannah and Lia. And if I waffled when the time came to mow my enemies down, then a half-blood like me would likely end up in the same state in short order.

I took a deep breath and narrowed my eyes at Hunter. I'd half expected him to attack again while my mind wandered, to force my hand until instinct morphed from defense to offense. But, instead, the uber-alpha seemed willing to bide his time and let me think the situation through rationally.

"Okay, I get it," I said quietly. The images in my mind and the turmoil in my gut were almost incomprehensible in our current location, surrounded by tall trees and gentle bird song. But I could smell a weasel that had passed through the clearing a few hours earlier, the tiny killer's breath salty with blood from an unlucky rabbit. In nature, I knew, nobody pulled their punches. And shifters were wolves as much as they were humans.

So when Hunter rushed me a second time, I met him with the full force of the sword in my hand. My opponent dodged aside, and I knew that even without the barrier formed by the current thin sheathe, my blade wouldn't have done more than shave a few hairs off the tip of his tail.

Faster, my wolf whispered. She had a good point, so rather than shush her, I invited her to join me up behind our shared eyes.

And this time when the uber-alpha rushed me, I could feel my lupine half tallying up the nearly invisible tension within our opponent's cord-like muscles. Together, we somehow knew that Hunter would dodge left, trying to draw our blade in that direction before sidestepping at the last moment and dashing between our legs.

So my wolf and I mirrored his approach. But rather than simply allowing the uber-alpha to advance unhindered, we stepped forward to meet him, feigning a block that would halt his left-handed pseudo-attack.

Then, at the last moment, we slid abruptly to the right, slamming our sword directly into the soft spot beneath our opponent's chin. The soft spot where Hunter's spine was least protected by fur and tough flesh.

The spot where a simple strike became a killing blow.

CHAPTER 18

"Fu..." I fumbled the word the same way I now fumbled my blade, dropping both to the forest floor. For a moment, I'd forgotten myself. Forgotten that I was training against a comrade while wielding a vicious hunk of metal that could slice a shifter in half. Forgotten my vow to protect my friends with my own life. Forgotten to hold back.

I fell to my knees, frantically parting the uber-alpha's hair to make sure he wasn't hurt. My heart was beating so fast I found it difficult to breathe and my throat was raw from my gasping breaths. *Let him be alright.*

Hunter shivered beneath my ministrations. And then there was a kneeling man in my arms rather than a hefty wolf. A kneeling man with a distinct lack of clothing to shield his taut skin from my frenzied fingers.

I'd ended up beside naked pack mates dozens of times in the past and the encounter was usually entirely innocent. Shifters often fell into bed as wolves then woke up human, with the result that they lacked the usual civilized modesty of two-leggers.

Other times, our nakedness had been shared and purposeful. But never had it felt anything like this.

"Once isn't enough," the uber-alpha murmured, his voice rough. "We need to keep at it until the killing stroke comes as naturally as breathing."

For a moment, I didn't know what he was referring to. But then I remembered our fight, my wolf's assistance, our lucky strike. Yes, Hunter was right—I needed to continue practicing with my sword if I wanted to be sure I could save Lia's life the next day.

But not right this instant. Not when my mate and I were alone with no possibility of interruption for the first time in the recent past and for the last time in the foreseeable future.

I took a deep breath of the pine-scented air and relaxed into the tranquil ambiance. Warm sunlight percolated gently through leaves above our heads, giving the impression of a frozen moment stolen from time. The glowing orb's gentle caresses loosened tense muscles and made me bold.

"Okay," I agreed. But I didn't release Hunter's nape from my grasp. Instead, I nudged his bent legs further apart and eased myself closer until we were almost chest-to-chest, he on his bare bum and I on my denim-coated knees. Using the hand that had been searching for injury along the base of his skull, I drew my companion in until I could whisper into his ear: "But first, I expect a reward for good behavior."

This was the second time I'd acted like a brazen hussy around Hunter and it wasn't lost upon me that the uber-alpha had never been the one to initiate physical contact between us in the past. But we were going into battle tomorrow, which made the concept of flirting coyly while hoping for reciprocation seem unbearably slow. What if one of us didn't make it out alive and I went to my grave never having shared more than a single kiss with this magnetic uber-alpha who had once called me his mate?

To the brave go the spoils, I thought, nibbling a line of seduction down Hunter's earlobe. My skin quivered with anticipation as I waited to see how the uber-alpha would respond.

Before, Hunter had acted hesitant every time I flung myself into his embrace. But not this time. Now, rock-hard arms glistening with sweat rose up to surround me and Hunter's scent enveloped my body like a heady cloud of warm perfume. I relaxed into the sassafras aroma as if resting by a warm fire on a cold winter night.

Irresistible.

The spicy scent cradled my chin and cheeks and, to my delight, Hunter's fingers soon followed suit. "Are you sure this is what you want?" he asked, rough calmes tickling across my skin as his fingers touched me lightly as butterfly wings.

In response, I reached up and stroked a lone finger across my companion's chiseled jaw. He hadn't taken the time to shave this morning, and the scratchy stubble of an incipient beard attempted to grab hold of my skin. I didn't mind—I felt exactly the same way. Putting so much as an inch between myself and my companion's magnetic pull was impossible.

"I don't want to lose you tomorrow," I whispered by way of reply, my voice husky with desire but my stomach hollowing out with fear. Unlike my wolf, I had a hard time believing we'd both make it out of tomorrow's battle unscathed.

"You won't lose me. If you let me in, I'll stay there." Hunter's words were a firm promise and he lifted me into his lap as easily as if I were a pine cone. I didn't miss the way my partner was shielding my skin from the rough debris on the forest floor even though I was the one who wore clothes while he didn't.

Yes, his chivalry was alluring. But it didn't quite knock me off the mental trail I'd been following even as I lowered my arm to trace a forefinger across the rope-like muscles that spanned his arm from shoulder to fingertip.

"But I have a pack to take care of," I elaborated. "And you said yourself that you don't understand packs."

There it was—the real roadblock that had been standing in our way this entire time. Even as the words left my mouth, I felt abruptly chilled, sweat evaporating from damp fabric clinging to my skin as an errant breeze drifted down through the canopy to ruffle my hair. I leaned far enough back in Hunter's arms so I could make out his eyes and I held my breath as I waited for his reply.

"I'll learn packs," Hunter rumbled easily. "They're important to you, so they're important to me."

His firm hands cupped my butt, rocking me gently forward until his hard length of manhood rubbed against my cleft. The seam of my pants pressed inward to chafe with exquisite agony against my most sensitive spot and I gasped out an "Oh!" of surprise.

For some unknown amount of time, I lost my train of thought as Hunter led us in an excruciating dance, all slow movement and sparks of tangled nerves and bodies. But he wasn't quite done with his promises yet.

"For you, I'll be nice to Ginger," Hunter murmured, his voice becoming huskier by the moment. "I'll bond with Cinnamon and Glen. And I'll free Lia if it's the last thing I do." His lips drifted down to taste and suck at my salty neck, the prickle of his beard sending me into a frenzy.

"Hunter..." I gasped, demanded. I was abruptly *done* with words and ready for his lips to become otherwise engaged. My exploring fingers turned into claws drawing him closer and I attempted to merge my mate's body with my own.

"You're right," Hunter concluded. "Now's not the time to talk about our pack."

Then I was abruptly shirtless, a breeze replacing my companion's questing fingers as the forest air encircled my exposed skin. I barely had time to shiver, though, before Hunter had pulled me back closer to his body, his hands sending frissons of pleasure across my sensitive belly as they hunted for the snap of my jeans.

I wanted to go there. But I pushed his fingers aside while murmuring a gentle rejection. "Not so fast, big guy."

Hunter had put me in the driver's seat here atop his body, and I wanted to take full advantage of the opportunity. Placing hands on his rock-hard shoulders to steady myself, I rotated my clad hips in slow circles atop his erection. Then I hummed with pleasure as the friction kindled swirling eddies of pleasure deep within my core.

I half expected my partner to flip me over onto my back and take the lead there and then. But, instead, he merely tilted up my chin so our gazes united once more. The uber-alpha's pupils were now so dilated with desire that his pale retinas were nearly non-existent, and I could have sworn I saw his wolf reflected in the dark depths within.

He swallowed me into a deep, bruising kiss. And only after we were both thoroughly breathless did he release my mouth long enough to whisper: "You're the boss. Do your worst."

Still, the bloodling's fingers continued to trail feather-light pathways across the exposed skin of my arms, my collarbone, my neck as if he couldn't quite bear to relinquish control. Goose bumps rose on my forearms as I struggled to focus on anything other than the needy ache that rose in my center in response to Hunter's caress.

But then my mate suited actions to words, leaning back on his elbows so I was given free rein to explore his body just as I'd requested. He was marvelous. All hard ridges and craggy folds, the power of his wolf nearly seeping out the seams to mesh with his human form.

I ran a tentative hand across my partner's muscular chest, abruptly unsure about what to do with this wolf who I'd apparently tamed. What to do with this power that Hunter had so easily granted me.

And then my own inner beast was there beside me. *We fit*, she whispered, pressing our splayed hands onto Hunter's chest to brace ourselves as we twisted and twined against him. Slowly, gently, my animal half guided me into a soft bump and grind until my passion was stoked back up to the boiling point and I was once again inflamed with desire. Soon, I was mewling needy little whimpers that had nothing to do with my inner wolf and had everything to do with the basest extreme of my own human nature.

It was only when jeans slid down off my body, one leg releasing then the other, that I realized my wolf was long gone and it was only Hunter and me dancing once more. My mate's fingers left trails of fire shimmering down my thighs, across my hips, eddying in circles around my breasts. And in response I reached forward with hungry hands, guiding Hunter's cock toward my slick opening.

"Shh, not quite yet." The uber-alpha had been willing to let me do as I pleased before. But now that the moment of truth was nigh, he didn't quite trust that I was adequately aroused. Instead, clever fingers slipped into my soft slit, gently teasing velvety skin as fingertips tested, tweaked, turned.

I writhed beneath his hand, quivering with need. Then foil tore and a condom encircled his throbbing shaft. Hunter had come prepared for more than simple sword fighting this morning.

I thought my partner, my mate, was less moved than I by this moment of exquisite joining. But then I heard his gasp turn into a moan as I slid down over his hard length, my center achingly sensitive and at the same time yearning to be filled. His mouth plundered mine and I gasped against his lips as our bodies and souls united.

"You...are...my...pack," he ground out as firm fingers bit into my buttocks. Then, he was pounding, pushing, feasting, sucking.

Our legs wound together as we rolled, and I hardly noticed the sharp leaf tips biting into my bare skin. It was impossible to tell who was leading and who was following now as each body engulfed the other.

Sassafras and sweat. Wolf and human.

We met. We merged.
We exploded.

CHAPTER 19

When I dragged my dirty, battered, and exhausted body back through the hotel-room door that afternoon, all I wanted was a shower. Hot water, fluffy towels, clean sheets—the promised trio sounded near miraculous after five hours of heavy sparring and the momentous pleasure that had come before.

But the expressions on my pack mates' faces proved that the comforts of home would have to wait. Flicking my attention from shifter to shifter, I traced their displeasure, anger, and worry back to its source.

At the epicenter of the discontent, I wasn't at all surprised to find Ginger holding her cell phone out toward me while shooting virtual daggers at my companion. Yep, our ill-fated vote yesterday hadn't done pack cohesion any favors.

When I saw the image on the trouble twin's small screen, though, I swallowed hard and stopped worrying about the two warring shifters' incompatibility. Because Ginger had found a photo of Lia, but the girl no longer looked like the happy, fresh-faced kid who had piled into our car as recently as yesterday morning. No, this Lia resembled a Holocaust survivor with a bloodied face, mussed hair, and haunted eyes. This Lia looked broken.

I fell backwards into a chair, unable to hold myself erect when faced with the reality of my own failure to protect my fellow shifters. *At least she's alive*, I reminded myself. Or Lia *had* been alive when the photo was taken. I averted my eyes from the phone, unable to meet the girl's eyes for a second longer.

"Push play," Ginger demanded. Only then did I notice what would have been obvious to anyone even a bit more tech savvy than I was. A little arrow within a circle smack dab in the center of the image proved that I was actually looking at the landing page for a video rather than at a still photo. Unfortunately, based on the heavy tension in the air around me, I didn't think I'd like what I was about to see any better than I'd liked the preview.

With trembling fingers, I tapped the play icon even as Hunter stepped up beside me. One warm hand fell onto my shoulder, but this time I had a feeling the uber-alpha was seeking support as much as giving it. And as we watched the young shifter on screen suck in a gasp that was almost a sob, Hunter's breathing turned similarly erratic beside me.

"Here you go, Talon. What do you think? An acceptable sacrifice?"

We couldn't see anyone other than Lia on screen, and the muffled male voice was digitally altered to hide the speaker's identity. Lia's captor could have been anyone.

Still, his words shot through me like fire. *Talon*. The exact same name Crew had mentioned as his sponsor within the SSS.

Now we know who we need to kill, my wolf growled deep within our shared belly. And I didn't even consider slapping her down. If this Talon was responsible for both Lia's kidnapping and for Crew's descent to the dark side, then my animal nature could be as bloodthirsty as she wanted in defense of our pack. We'd find out who Talon was, and together we'd take him down.

Then my blood ran cold because Lia spoke at last. And the single word that emerged from the girl's split lips wasn't one that I'd expected to hear in a million years. *"Hunter,"* she moaned.

I shook my head, trying to dislodge the sound from my brain. No, I must have picked that up wrong. It wasn't possible.

As my stomach sank into my boots, I stared up at the shifter standing inches away from me. The shifter who'd made love to me today with—I'd thought—powerful feelings that matched my own. The shifter who'd fought by Lia's side at the campground yesterday morning and who had seemed honestly concerned about Cinnamon's fate a few hours later.

Over and over again, I'd given the uber-alpha the benefit of the doubt despite the evidence stacking up against him. As Ginger had pointed out so acerbically, Hunter had repeatedly shown up at decidedly suspicious moments. He'd admitted to seeing no point in a pack, and yet he'd stuck around to ingratiate himself into the good graces of both the halfies within our little group—me and Lia—while roundly ignoring everyone else. He'd even cast me out of my old clan, for crying out loud, ensuring that I had no way to protect myself from his machinations.

And what had I done in response? I'd bent over backwards to make up excuses for the uber-alpha's behavior. He was a bloodling, I told myself, and not especially socially adroit. He was employed by the Tribunal to hunt down the SSS, so of course he'd be poking around in the land of the missing halfies.

He had a good heart.

That's gotta be my weakest effort at voluntary stupidity to date, I berated myself. After all, hadn't I only begun trusting Hunter after he used the four-letter M word? Was I really so desperate that I'd accepted the first psychopath who gave me the time of day?

Yep. Yep, apparently I was.

Or at least, I *had* been. Now, I pushed myself out of the chair so violently that it fell over, one hard wooden leg banging against Hunter's bruised shins in the process. My companion winced, but remained standing tall and firm, waiting for me to draw the inevitable conclusion from the evidence placed before me.

I opened my mouth, but found I was unable to speak. Instead, my body vibrated with pain as if Hunter were biting into me once again, just as he'd done to catch my attention in the forest earlier that day. Only this time around, his sharp lupine teeth seemed to move up and settle around my chest, pushing all air out of my lungs and spearing my heart.

I wanted to wail and moan at the agony, but instead I pierced the uber-alpha with an angry gaze. For some crazy reason, Hunter had his head cocked to one side in a gesture of hopeful expectation. As if he was waiting for me to denounce the evidence I'd heard with my own two ears.

Do you really think I can forgive this? I roared silently. And Hunter took a step backwards as if struck. But he still made no move to leave.

We might have stood there frozen in our silent battle forever if Ginger hadn't intervened. Her words cut through the emotions that hung like foul smoke in the hotel-room air. And as she spoke, I finally found myself able to take in one shuddering breath after another. "Now do you finally understand what I've been trying to tell you?" my pack mate demanded.

"Yes," I replied simply, not taking my eyes off the uber-alpha. It was his strength that had attracted me to him in the first place, I decided. The uber-alpha was so absurdly powerful that I'd trusted my untrustworthy wolf and accepted the comfort of his protection. In the process, I'd closed my eyes to the truth, had believed Hunter's lies, and had lost a pack mate in the process.

Not lost, my wolf whispered. *We'll find Lia.*

I hoped so, but couldn't really see how. Not when the uber-alpha before us was implicated in her kidnapping and had been privy to every stage of our recovery plan to date.

For a moment, I considered ordering my pack to pile on, to take Hunter down and force Lia's location out of him. But we didn't stand a chance against the uber-alpha's root-beer dominance. He'd bark out a single command and we'd all wither away to nothing, starving to death within arm's reach of a mini fridge chock full of caloric leftovers.

In fact, I realized now that I was well and truly stuck. The best I could hope for was to squash my wolf in an effort to make myself immune to Hunter's incalculable dominance then mow the uber-alpha down with the sword that was still belted at my hip. The strategy wouldn't help us find Lia, but it *would* prevent the traitor from actively working against us as we continued our efforts to free our pack's youngest member.

No! My wolf rebelled, but it took only a blink of an eye to thrust her down into the dark recesses of my mind, deeper than I'd ever sent her before. Let the inner beast battle those monsters of loneliness, lack of belonging, and back-stabbing mates for a while. Maybe she'd do some good and my nightmares would become a little less frequent in the future.

Then I whipped my weapon out of its scabbard, glad that I'd pulled the so-called condom off the blade during the ride back to the hotel. *And why didn't Hunter simply take me hostage then when we were alone if he's just trying to up his halfie count?* I wondered. *Why flirt with me and train me and fuck me senseless?*

The issue was irrelevant. Lia had spoken as if Hunter was present in her prison cell, and I had to trust information from our pack's youngest member over the yearnings of my own heart.

Still, with my back to the other shifters in the room, I mouthed the word "Go" at my opponent. Even now, I didn't want to use the killing strokes he'd taught me in order to skewer a man who I'd caressed with such wild abandon mere hours earlier. Some traitorous part of my mind still wanted to believe that I was wrong in my re-analysis of my mate.

My mate. I closed my eyes for a split second to regather my composure. And when I pried my lids back up, Hunter's clothes lay in a puddle on the carpeted floor.

But the uber-alpha himself was gone.

CHAPTER 20

Twenty-four hours of relentless scrabbling for another solution turned up no new leads, so we arrived at the farmer's field the next afternoon with very little hope but with an outsized dose of determination. Surely Hunter would have simply moved the ceremony to another location after being busted for complicity. Or perhaps he was busy setting up a trap to reel us back in and would be thrilled when we stupidly showed our faces right where he expected us to be.

But the online front for the SSS that Ginger had tracked down the day before was sketchy at best, suggesting that perhaps the uber-alpha didn't have a direct line of communication with his underlings after all. Perhaps the loose-knit group of shifters hadn't learned how to build a phone tree and thus had no way of getting in touch with each other save turning up every Friday evening to howl together at the moon. And perhaps Hunter, like us, would simply be forced to arrive and hope he'd be able to take down as many halfies as possible in the face of our clan's moderate show of offensive strength.

Perhaps I'll start answering to the name Pollyanna too, I thought uncomfortably as I stepped out of our clan's car. I couldn't quite believe that I was leading my pack mates into danger with my eyes wide open to the stupidity of the endeavor. But I also couldn't imagine staying home and ignoring the chance—no matter how slender—that Lia would be gutted tonight on this very field. No, as stupid as it was to show up, it would be stupider to stay away.

"I'm coming in with you," Cinnamon said as the other three shifters joined me outside the vehicle's metal walls. As directed, the male trouble twin had parked down a narrow lane that was nearly invisible from the main road but that was only a short jaunt upwind from the location Quill had scouted out the day before. This was the moment of truth, ten minutes before sunset...and already my pack was rebelling.

"You're our getaway driver," I reminded Cinnamon, but the male trouble twin—who was usually gentle and humorous—just growled a rejection of my reiteration of his role. He wanted to be part of the strike force and he didn't seem willing to take no for an answer.

The truth was that Ginger's brother *was* doing better after two days of forced rest. He'd healed enough that sitting upright was no longer a struggle, and his wounds had stopped oozing every time he moved an arm or a leg funny. Still, everyone but Cinnamon himself knew that the male trouble twin would be a liability rather than an asset on the mission ahead.

So I elaborated, trying to smooth the shifter's ruffled fur. "You have an important job to do," I reminded him. "If we can tear Lia and Savannah away from the SSS and get them to you, then at least we'll know the two innocents are safe. The rest of us can take care of ourselves. But you saw the video—Lia might not be able to walk. She *needs* you to be ready to spirit her out of the line of fire."

"I can do that and still come in with you," Cinnamon argued. But he hadn't risen from the driver's seat yet, clear evidence that the male was still too weak to join us on the battleground.

I sighed, preparing to muster a little alpha dominance and force the malleable shifter to toe the line. But Ginger took her brother in hand before I could speak up again.

"Do I have to handcuff you to the steering wheel?" the female demanded, dangling the restraints that we'd brought along for an entirely different purpose through her brother's open window. The young woman was revved up and ready to rumble, and her wolf was so rampant that I could almost see its image superimposed over her human skin as she spoke. Neither Cinnamon nor I doubted that she really would cuff her brother to the wheel if he didn't toe the line.

So I didn't have to expend my weak powers to get Cinnamon to play it safe after all. "No, ma'am," the male trouble twin said, eyes submissively trained on our feet as he backed down. Then he muttered, "Be careful."

"Always am and nothing bad's happened to me yet," Ginger agreed. She shed clothes as she spoke, and then the female trouble twin fell onto paws with a speed that nearly rivaled the traitorous uber-alpha's. Beside her, Glen's wolf form caught my eye and then nudged his current partner to get her moving away from the car. The pair curved into the trees as a unit, moving into place as planned so they'd be ready when the enemy shifters arrived.

Quill, Cinnamon, and I, on the other hand, remained resolutely human. It was hard for me to wait two-legged even though my weak wolf would provide little additional offensive power, but she and I both knew this was an integral part of our plan.

So I forced myself to unclasp the sword belt from around my waist and hand the weapon into the car to Cinnamon for safekeeping. In for a penny, in for a pound.

And now I'm both unarmed and thin-skinned. I shivered, knowing the unvarnished assessment of my current state was far too true. Without the aid of my katana, I had no chance of fighting free if the enemy saw through our little charade.

Focus. The word breathed from wolf to human mind and back to animal again. Inhaling deeply, we calmed our pounding pulse together. Then, through the trees, we heard the first car door slam.

One door, then another. A crunch of tires on gravel, then more metal on metal. *Two vehicles,* I thought. *One for Lia and one for Savannah.*

I reached toward my wolf, hoping to borrow her nose to gather a little additional olfactory feedback. It would be handy to know how many enemies we faced and whether both of the kidnapped halfies were present before I donned the handcuffs that Ginger had threatened her brother with a few minutes earlier.

"Only two enemies," Cinnamon murmured. "Lia's there, and one other female—young, weak, probably Savannah. We could take them down with a frontal assault if you'd let me help...."

My pack mate's words trailed off as I shook my head and turned around so my back was facing Quill. "We can't risk Lia getting injured before we reach them," I disagreed, mouth muffled against the side of the car.

Then, allowing the cowboy shifter to fasten hard metal handcuffs around my unresisting wrists, my own partner and I strode together toward the meeting grounds of the enemy who held our pack mate's life in their unyielding hands.

CHAPTER 21

I could neither smell nor see Hunter, but I got the distinct impression that he was out there four-legged, watching and waiting as my pack and I moved into position. His presence was akin to a tingle at the base of my spine, the same sensation that I'd experienced over and over again during the last twenty-four hours of jittery anticipation. I'd kept looking over my shoulder all day long, in fact, expecting Hunter to return for his clothes, wallet, and SUV. But instead the uber-alpha appeared to have turned wolf and disappeared from our lives as quickly and as thoroughly as he'd come into them.

And yet, if my overactive nerve endings were any indication, Hunter hadn't really abandoned us at all—just taken a step back until we couldn't quite see him out of the corners of our eyes. Whether the sensation was the work of the pack bond or just wishful thinking on my part, though, didn't really matter. Either Hunter really was my mate and we were in good shape —with five able-bodied shifters and a recovering getaway driver toeing off against two SSS members—or the uber-alpha was merely waiting to turn the tide of the battle in the opposite direction and ensure that we all perished.

Regardless, I couldn't do anything about it now. In fact, as soon as I set eyes on my youngest pack mate, I immediately forgot everything except the urge to rush closer to the girl as quickly as possible.

Lia had already been pulled out of one of the cars by the time I caught sight of her and she was now being dragged over to where the other outpack male waited with his hand firmly clamped onto the shoulder of a second prisoner. Our youngest pack mate had every right to be cowed after days of confinement, but Lia was instead holding her shit together with a strength of will that would have made her cousins proud. The girl's cheeks were tear-stained, but her chin jutted skyward as she dug her heels into the dirt and roundly refused to give in to her captor's attempts to move her along.

Savannah, on the other hand, looked nearly comatose. Or at least I assumed the other girl was Savannah. I wouldn't have recognized the teenager from her photo, smiles and youthful charm having been completely obliterated by dirt and bruises. And unlike Lia, Savannah was hunched over as if her kidneys hurt. Her wolf was clearly too quiescent to give the girl the boost she needed to survive any further ordeal.

I wanted to swear and then tear into the two males who were manhandling the kidnapped girls with such disregard for their captives' humanity. But that wasn't the plan. Instead, Quill and I paced forward, purposefully coming upon the group aslant and from downwind, so the enemy wouldn't notice us until we were almost close enough to touch.

The night before, the pack and I had gone back and forth over the issue of Quill's presence on the front line of the upcoming showdown. Would the outpack males who we were hoping to ambush have been in the bar Tuesday night, meaning they would have seen the cowboy shifter leave with us? Or could he pass as just another SSS member that Lia's captors didn't happen to know personally?

"I'll make them believe," Quill had promised, raising one eyebrow at me as if asking my future permission to knock his new pack leader around. Now he made good on that past promise, loudly rebuking me for my supposed dilly-dallying, then shoving me so hard that I nearly fell to the earth at his feet.

The abrupt greeting appeared to have worked. I couldn't actually see the SSS males' faces since my bound hands prevented me from catching myself before I slammed into the side of the nearest car. But the strangers' voices were congratulatory as they greeted what they assumed was another halfie-hunting shifter showing up with his catch at the usual Friday night watering hole.

And even though I'd banged myself up good during our introduction to the scene, I was glad that Quill's quick thinking had kept my face averted from the SSS crew. Unlike the cowboy shifter with his impressive acting skills, I has having a hard time maintaining a disheartened demeanor. Instead, I felt triumphant as I realized that our plan was actually going off without a hitch.

This was it. We'd edged ourselves close enough to Lia and Savannah so we could now pull the girls out of harm's way before the rest of our pack mates joined in the fight. Soon, both kids would be tucked away in bed with soup and hot chocolate and whatever else we could think of to lull them back into a very real sense of security. Soon, our entire pack would once again be fully united.

But then the shifter holding Lia burst my bubble with a single word. "Nice work, Talon," he said. "I didn't really think you could do it, but you managed after all. A halfie alpha!"

Talon! Absurdly, I wasted a split second thinking I must have been mistaken. Quill was a nice guy, a thoughtful member of our crew. He was here to help Lia escape.

To help Lia who had formed a supposedly irrational dislike of our newest member as soon as he entered our lives? No, Quill/Talon was present for one purpose and one purpose alone. To increase the SSS's weekly haul, bringing in not only two weak girls but also a third half-blood shifter whose wolf was equally lily-livered but who had been granted an unusual power by a friendly pack leader.

If, as I suspected, the SSS was somehow stealing their prey's lupine capabilities each time they murdered a half-blood, then I was the holy grail. A halfie weak enough to easily sacrifice on the altar, but with a hidden strength that would boost the outpack males' own wolves far more effectively than the spirits of the other two girls currently in their grasp.

"Glen, Ginger, attack!" I screamed, struggling against my captor's grasp and hoping my pack mates would be able to descend upon the enemy quickly enough to wrest the two teenagers out of the outpack males' control. But instead I heard Lia's shriek of rage becoming muffled as a car door slammed and shut her away from the outside world. Then I felt the prick of a needle invading my bicep as the world turned fuzzy around me.

"You were so easy to manipulate," Quill whispered in my ear. "So easy to catch."

And then the world went black.

CHAPTER 22

I awoke in a hole in the ground. And, in case you're a *Hobbit* fan, let me assure you—it *was* a nasty, dirty, wet hole, filled with the ends of worms and an oozy smell. Plus, my prison was as dark as the grave.

Perhaps it *was* my grave.

The image of dying there, with no pack mates around to mourn me, filled my mind. I'd rot alone in this hole, my bones jumbling together as carrion beetles rolled my flesh into tiny balls to feed to their offspring. Snakes would slither down to capture the tiny critters drawn to feed upon my decomposing flesh and tree roots would eventually invade the pockets of fertility left behind.

At least then I'd be good for something.

I shuddered, my head pounding as I tried to push through the drugged fog and remember what had happened back in that farmer's field.

The turncoat, the needle prick, the car doors slamming...I'd obviously been captured, but surely Lia and Savannah had gotten away?

No, I distinctly remembered my youngest pack mate's screams as she was forced into the vehicle nearest me. Thought I might have recalled her cradling my comatose body against her own slender form as we sped out of the lot, my head jiggling nervelessly on my neck just before unconsciousness fully claimed me.

If Lia and Savannah were prisoners like I was, then I needed to find and help them.

"Is anyone there?" I whispered into the darkness, reaching my hands out in search of other living beings. One arm grazed a skinny, damp object that might have been a root...or a severed finger. I jerked away, hitting my head on a protruding rock in the process of reeling backwards into the void.

My stomach was too queasy to risk opening my mouth even so far as to swear. Instead, I held perfectly still, listening to the way my breathing echoed within my ears. Hyperventilation was soothing in its own way, I decided. The heaving breaths proved I was still alive, that the earth hadn't yet swallowed me whole.

Get it together.

My wolf's whisper shook me out of the mindless terror I was falling into, and I didn't even care that she'd joined me behind our shared eyes without invitation. It wasn't as if there was anything for her to see in the pitch black hole anyway.

"Look for escape," she whispered aloud with my lips. And I nodded, proving that I really was crazy—not only talking to myself but replying as well. *Right, escape.*

I patted myself down first, finding that I was still wearing the clothes I'd started out the day in. Or perhaps that had been the day before? With no light in my hole, I didn't know if it was today or tomorrow—and now I was just confusing myself with my own words. The pounding headache didn't help matters either.

Focus. Surely I have some weapons left.

My trembling fingers brushed across jeans and t-shirt, found Crew's collar still stashed away in one bulging pocket. I'd never gotten around to examining the item, I now realized, never taken the time to decipher the source of the rotten-banana odor that had allowed the SSS shifters to break through Hunter's iron grip.

Well, now I've got all the time in the world. That wasn't really true— even in my somewhat altered state, I realized that Quill wouldn't just leave me down in this hole to molder. No, the outpack male had likely stashed all three of us halfies away for safekeeping until the time was ripe to rip out our hearts like he'd harvested organs from the unfortunate Daisy Rambler. I might have days, hours, or only minutes alone. Best get to the task of escaping.

This would have been easier in daylight, I grumbled. But the wolf only snorted within my skin and brought our shared hands up so we could sniff at the collar while running light fingers down its length. There was the faintest hint of rotten banana yet present, the odor emanating from a little plastic indentation that currently held the smallest iota of moisture.

What do you think? I asked my animal half, then waited what seemed like an eternity for a reply that never came.

She was gone, I realized. Even the barest essence of rotten banana remaining had been enough to momentarily banish my wolf. Which meant I *did* have the tiniest ace in the hole—a way to force myself out of an alpha compulsion, if necessary.

Assuming, of course, that I was able to pull the collar out of my pocket and bring it up to my nose while a shifter stronger than me tried to force my muscles to act otherwise. Not likely.

Pushing the collar back into my pocket, I fought down the terror that threatened to rise back up in my throat now that my animal half had gone missing. Wolf or no wolf, I wasn't a damsel in distress and the collar wasn't my only possible escape hatch. There was the tracking device for one....

Fingers slipped down toward my left sock, seeking the tiny sliver of plastic and metal that Glen had purchased as an auxiliary safety measure. *"We'll be able to find you anywhere there's satellite reception,"* my stalwart second had promised, his veiled eyes doing their best not to ask me to think up a strategy that didn't involve being taken back to the enemy's lair as bait.

In all fairness, that hadn't actually been my plan. The tracking device was for backup only.

Or it *had* been for backup. Because my frantic fingers found no bump beneath my left sock. And when I tried the other ankle, hoping my drug-addled brain had just forgotten precisely where I stashed the device, no chunk of plastic turned up there either.

I closed my eyes, allowing the voluntary darkness to erode away the newfound rush of adrenaline that was threatening to turn me into a quivering mass of jelly. *Breathe*, I reminded myself, wishing my wolf would show back up to keep me company.

It was no big surprise the tracking device was gone. After all, Quill had been privy to its installation just as he'd been privy to every other aspect of our planning process.

Won't Ginger be pissed when she realizes she went after the wrong outpack male after all?

I tried to smile but was pretty sure the expression on my face was closer to a grimace. *Okay, so no one will be riding to the rescue. No biggie. I'll just find my own way out.*

I stretched out a tentative arm once more, this time steeling myself to face the slimy, unknown objects that met my touch. *It's like being in a haunted house, I told myself. A kid plunges his hands into a vat in the dark and is sure he's fingering entrails. But the lights come on and it's just spaghetti.*

Somehow, though, I didn't think the nasty, slithery objects around me were spaghetti.

Not the point, I rebutted my own rebuttal. *The point is to figure out where my prison cell starts and ends so I can find a way out. Remember— it's up to me to rescue Lia.*

Even the faint memory of the girl's prideful chin as she was yanked away from the SSS member's car made me smile. And my upturned lips in turn gave me strength to reach out again to feel the walls of my prison.

I didn't even have to stretch, it turned out, because the hole I was imprisoned within must have been dug in a hurry. It was rounded at the bottom, with clods of dirt littered here and there, and the total width was less than the length of a single arm.

That's a good thing, I told myself, ignoring my childlike fear of the close, dark space. *It means I can brace myself against the far wall and climb back out.*

I straightened, preparing to suit action to words...and hit my head painfully on a wooden ceiling.

Could it really be so easy? Just push off the lid and pop up like a jack-in-the-box? Putting my back into it, I spread both hands across the damp boards and pushed with all my might.

The ceiling didn't so much as budge. The hatch was either locked tight or covered with an object so heavy there was no way I could dislodge it.

Or maybe I really am buried alive.

My heart rate began to pick up, but I refused to be defeated so easily. Taking a deep breath, I decided: *So I'll carve my way out around the edges instead.*

Glad my fingernails were cut short, I scrabbled at the earth beside the wooden ceiling. Dirt fell into my hair, caught in my eyes, and settled around my feet. Blinking painfully against the invasive particles, I cupped my fingers into mole-like claws and dug yet harder.

A tiny stone tore at the soft flesh of one cuticle, but I paid it no mind. Splinters embedded themselves in my skin as I continued to disinter more of the wooden boards that topped my lair, but it was too dark to see if I bled. I yanked the offending slivers of wood out with my teeth and kept going.

Further and further I dug. I *would* break through.

Only when I'd filled the entire bottom of my prison cell with six inches of debris and the air had grown decidedly moldy from a dislodged I-didn't-want-to-think-about-what-it-was did I pause. I'd carved out an indentation on one side of the wooden ceiling large enough to fill with my head and shoulders. In other words, I'd created just a hair more breathing room...but there was no sign of daylight creeping through the cracks and the boards above my head felt never-ending.

I'll never see daylight again.

I tried to breathe, tried to swallow down the massive knot in my throat. But I couldn't even force myself to bend my knees and settle back into the dirt. Instead, I shifted forms without meaning to, my wolf emerging tangled in a mess of human clothing.

Caught, tight, stuck.

Terror-stricken, I lashed out at the bonds that held me in place.

Then, relief, as my animal spirit woke and pushed my human brain aside. Pushed my consciousness back down into her lupine belly. Took complete command of the body that we no longer shared, that she had instead claimed for her very own.

Happily, I sank into a new kind of darkness.

CHAPTER 23

"Fen, are you out there? I feel you. Where are you?"

Lia's voice echoed in my mind as I reentered consciousness. I opened gritty lupine eyes, but still saw nothing. Stretched my nose until it bumped into the same dank wall, only the surface was wetter this time around than it had been before. Plus, I was now paw-deep in a soup of mud rather than in loose earth. Perfect, my hole had become not only small and dark, but also out-and-out wet.

Raining outside, my animal half suggested, soothing me as if I were a child. *But, smell—fresh air coming in.*

Sure enough, the wolf was right. With her enhanced senses, I could feel the faintest eddy of air flowing into our prison cell through cracks in the earthen walls and the boards overhead. The urge to try one more time to dig ourselves free nearly overwhelmed me.

Unfortunately, my previous attempt at emulating a mole had resulted in the wolf taking complete command of our body for who knows how long. So maybe that wasn't such a great idea after all.

Small, tight, trapped.

I whined aloud, almost dropping out of consciousness as claustrophobia set back in with a vengeance. This time, though, my wolf buoyed me up and refused to allow me to drift down into the void.

Shh, she whispered. *We'll be alright.*

I only realized the sound had carried across the pack bond when Lia's voice once again entered my mind. *"Fen?"* The girl's tone had been desperate before, but now she was even more frantic. So much so that I thought I could actually smell her fright and feel the sweat beading on her forehead.

While I'd like to say the sensation focused my attention on my pack mate's predicament, her fear instead exacerbated my own fight-or-flight reaction. My breathing turned harsh and as I contemplated overwhelming my animal partner just long enough to drift back down inside her lupine belly. I could let the wolf deal with the water slowly creeping up around our furry ankles. I could let the wolf deal with a terrified pack mate who wasn't physically present but who must have been close by in order to reach me through the pack bond. I could let the wolf take full command of the situation.

I've already failed. What's the point of banging my head against the wall over and over again?

"Fen!" This time, the agitation in Lia's tone had been replaced with excitement. *"I'm so glad you're awake! I've been feeling your wolf for hours. But she's not so good at words, and I thought I might be dreaming the whole thing...."*

And there was that vision of Lia's prideful chin once again. Of the halfie valiantly leading SSS wolves toward the medusa-like gaze of the uber-alpha without worrying about the risk to her own flesh and bones. If Lia was so brave without any extra alpha energy to call upon, then how could I be less so when I bore Wolfie's gift like a mantle protecting me from harm?

So I squashed my fear of the close, dark space. I squashed my own feelings of failure. And I got to work. *"Are you alone?"* I thought as loudly as I could, hoping the words would transmit down the invisible pack bond.

Abruptly, a brilliant line illuminated the air, the starlight and magic of the connection seeming to pierce the darkness...but not actually brightening the space in which I sat. Still, the thread of fluorescence gave me at least a modicum of information—that Lia was located off to my left, and that none of the rest of my clan was within communication range. Because the only other line of starlight beyond the one connecting me to my fellow prisoner was the thin umbilical cord through which Wolfie's alpha abilities subtly bolstered my own.

"No, I'm not alone. They have me and Savannah together," Lia answered, sounding like a young recruit enthusiastically reporting in to her drill sergeant. Her entire emotional signature had changed as soon as I took control of the situation, and I could almost see the girl raising one hand in the air in a military salute.

It was so easy to pep up the young—to make Lia believe I was strong enough to save her from a horror I couldn't even elude on my own behalf, let alone break another free of. Too bad it wasn't equally easy to bolster my own lack of self esteem.

Careful, my wolf whispered. But I shook our shared head, rejecting the animal's admonition. No, she needn't worry. I wasn't going down the oh-poor-me path again, not with Lia listening in. One pity party per hole in the ground was sufficient.

"What do your surroundings look like?" I asked Lia instead. I got the distinct impression that the more she communicated, the better she felt. And her growing good spirits buoyed up my own.

Plus, we'd need some sort of weapon to aid in our eventual escape. The wolf and I didn't seem likely to find one within our earth-walled pit, our meager stores having already been depleted by our recent jaunt into fur form. While I'd been comatose, in fact, my lupine half had wriggled her way out of all of our clothing save some now-stretched-out panties...which was a good thing for the sake of our emotional health, but not so much for the sake of our belongings. I was pretty sure that Crew's collar had been washed clean by the water rising up around our feet, so even that long shot was now absent from our arsenal. Hopefully Lia's surroundings would prove more productive.

"We're in a locked room," she began....

Then, abruptly, I could see out through the girl's eyes. The dim but present light from a small lamp settled into my belly like a balm, and it took me a solid minute to gather my focus enough to pay attention to details.

There was Savannah, conked out on a metal cot, the thin mattress lacking any blanket or pillow. Her hands and feet were bound, but no gag covered her mouth. So the girls were probably stashed somewhere far enough away from civilization that the SSS was unconcerned about strangers hearing their prisoners scream.

Unfortunately, this close to the vast expanse of the national forest, that didn't narrow our location down much at all.

"Show me the rest," I requested. Obediently, Lia's gaze panned slowly around the small space as if she were filing its contents away for later perusal. I saw a commode and a sink, although how the girls were supposed to use either with their hands tied behind their backs was beyond me.

The only object that looked remotely weapon-like was a pencil. *"Can you slide that into your waistband?"* I asked, and Lia promptly obeyed.

Not that a thin piece of wood and graphite was going to help us out much in the struggle ahead. What we really needed was an exit point, but the room boasted no windows and only a single door.

"Locked?" I asked. Even hog-tied, I was pretty sure Lia possessed the spunk necessary to check out all of her options.

"Yeah," she answered dispiritedly.

And yet, even as the girl sent her words down the pack bond, the knob began to turn. Slowly enough to feel like the entrance of the lead monster in a horror movie, the door cracked open to reveal a familiar face.

Not Hunter, of course, but Quill. The cowboy shifter looked even more put together than he had while slumming it with our pack, and I realized that his drifter persona had been just that—an act. As my wolf had tried to point out at the time, the male's van with the perfectly clean countertops and lack of clutter had likely been delivered by an SSS buddy to shore up his intended characterization as a lonely outpack male. I should have guessed that Quill had never roughed it a day in his life.

"Why would you have expected Hunter?" Lia asked me, confused by the hints of emotion that had filtered down our shared line. But even though the girl sent her words in my direction, her eyes remained trained on the SSS member whose smile sent a tremor down both of our spines. There was nothing pleasant about Quill's anticipated pleasure.

"Because you said his name," I explained. *"Ginger found the video...."*

The pack bond broadcast images from my end to Lia's in an instant. The showdown in the hotel room, the expression on Hunter's face when he saw a bloodied Lia and heard his own name dripping from her cracked and swollen lips.

Despite myself, my own feelings showed through as well, my pain and humiliation at having believed in a shifter who would dare to harm the youngest member of our pack. How I hadn't even been able to bear the sight as my anger chased away a male who I'd thought was my mate. How I hadn't seen him since.

"But Hunter wasn't there," Lia exclaimed. *"I was saying his name because it gave me the strength to go on. Because I thought he'd find me if I called out loudly enough. To help me escape."*

Then our communication was abruptly cut short as Quill demanded Lia's full attention. "Do you want to be first?" he asked, posing an unanswerable question. "Or should I wake Sleeping Beauty over there and see how well her heart goes with tonight's dinner of liver and onions instead?"

***

No way was I going to let either Lia or Savannah be injured on my watch, not if I had another way to counteract Quill's evil intentions. And I realized as I looked out through my pack mate's eyes that I *did* have a way to stall at least. I should be able to draw the SSS member to me and away from the easy pickings he was now perusing with such an avaricious gleam in his eyes. In the process—with a little luck—I might also buy the rest of our friends time to track us down.

Assuming I could summon help via the pack bond, that was. But I'd cross that bridge when I came to it.

Instead of focusing on the unknowable, I forced words out of Lia's mouth. "Don't you think *I'd* taste a little better than these skinny kids?"

The girl's head jerked as her tongue fumbled a sentence she hadn't planned on emitting, the words alien in her mouth. To our shared ears, the question sounded a little like Lia and a little like me, a strange combination of her voice and my intonation.

But Quill didn't notice the distinction at first, nor the unusual plural. Instead, he reached out, grabbing Lia's arm roughly and jerking her upright. "So good of you to volunteer."

Time to really get the bastard's attention. "Do you think this is what Faye would have wanted?" I demanded. I was pretty sure Quill hadn't taken the time to confide in Lia about his dead mate—if the female was even real— so evoking her name now should be enough to prove my presence. And maybe the memory would also remind our enemy of his nearly absent humanity as well.

Sure enough, the cowboy shifter was shocked into momentary stillness. Then he narrowed his eyes. "Fen? Is that you?"

I nodded Lia's head, hoping the kid didn't end up scarred for life due to this short-term possession. "Yes, I'm really this powerful," I taunted him. "Too bad you won't be the one to tear out my heart and take that power for your very own."

"What do you mean I won't be the one...?" Quill's voice trailed off as he came to the same conclusion I'd hoped he would—that one of his compatriots had decided to sneak around behind his back and make off with the greater prize while Quill was busy checking on the younger prisoners.

"Who's there with you?" he demanded. When I didn't speak, he slapped Lia's face hard in retaliation. My pack mate and I both cringed away from the sensation of warm blood drizzling down the girl's chin, her bottom lip resplitting where it had barely started to scab over. The cut burned.

"I'm sorry," I whispered, this time for my pack mate's ears alone. *"But I need to buy us some wiggle room so our friends can find us. And you probably won't be able to hear me soon. Will you be alright on your own?"*

"Of course," the girl answered, her chin nudging upwards once again.

She was so much braver than I was. Even as I began to draw away, Lia still stood strong and tall on her shackled feet.

In contrast, my lupine form was already huddling into the corner of the pit, pressing our sodden and matted fur into the mud in an effort to disappear. We could almost feel Quill's lupine teeth ripping through our skin.

Worse, my human mind was already reeling from the imagined future agony that would flare up when I put the other facet of my plan into action.

But I didn't let any of that terror color my words when I spoke mind-to-mind with my youngest pack mate for the last time. *"Good,"* I told Lia.

"I'm proud of you." Then I watched Quill slam back out of my friend's prison cell before I retreated into the quietude of my own mind.

CHAPTER 24

Wolf, I called softly. *I need your help.*

Obediently, my animal half rose up to join me. *What's the plan?* she murmured, her voice nearly too quiet to hear.

We'll try the easy way first, I replied. *But if all else fails, we'll break the unbreakable and see what happens.*

The wolf sipped my intentions out of our shared mind as if they were a long drink of cool water. Then she hummed her assent. *It's worth it,* she agreed, *to save Lia.*

Of course it was worth it. I closed our shared eyes and inhaled a few deep breaths, then reached out with as much force as I could muster in search of the tangle of intangible energy that bound me to my pack mates.

There was Lia, alone once more. And now that I pushed more energy into the effort I could also catch my pack mate's connection to the sleeping

Savannah. Lia had obviously taken the other girl under her wing and connected her cell mate to our clan through sheer force of will.

Good job, Lia, I whispered to myself. And I almost thought I saw the girl smile in reaction although I'd made no effort to push my words down our shared line.

But those weren't the shifters I was looking for. Instead, I visualized Glen, my most stout-hearted and steadfast companion. The lone male who had abandoned his chosen clan for no reason other than to protect my back. I could almost touch this firm friend with my human fingertips even though I currently wore paws. Could almost taste his scent on the air.

But I couldn't. Not quite.

Frustrated, I growled into the darkness. Glen must be too far away for our more moderate tether to access. Which meant Ginger was my best bet for mind-to-mind contact.

The female trouble twin and I'd had our disagreements of late, but our connection had previously appeared the strongest of anyone's in the pack. I brought to mind the young woman's smile as she danced atop the bar table. The glint of mischief and simple joy in her eyes as she—I now realized—tried to capture the attention of an elusive pack leader rather than—as I'd then assumed—catering to the libidos of a roomful of outpack males. Surely the friendship we'd built combined with Ginger's dreams of something more would help me reach the young woman even from this distance as long as I concentrated hard enough.

I sank my muzzle down onto my paws, trying to relax into the pack bond. But the puddled water had risen too high and I inhaled a choking noseful of muddy water by mistake. Coughing, I sprang to my feet and jabbed my hip hard against another stone jutting out of the rough walls of the pit.

This is stupid, I berated myself. *I should be putting every ounce of energy I've got into escape rather than fighting for alpha powers I don't know how to use.*

Hunter, my wolf rebutted.

Sighing, I admitted that my animal half was right. I'd already tried physical escape, so contacting the uber-alpha was my only remaining option.

If bond strength was anything to go by, in fact, I should have called out to my newest pack mate first. Now, remembering the bright thread of light that had connected me to the Tribunal enforcer, I wondered how I could have ever doubted that he really was my mate...and that I was more closely intertwined with Hunter's animal half than I was with any other member of our clan.

Okay, that wasn't quite true. Not the mate bond part—no, I was finally willing to admit that I'd made a supreme error in judgment sending Hunter away. He'd obviously been trying to protect me all week long, and his strong set of teeth might have provided the power necessary to sway yesterday's outcome in the other direction.

Sorry, Hunter, I whispered to no one. *I screwed up.*

Past mistakes aside, though, there *was* one other shifter who I could be confident of contacting quickly and definitively. One other shifter who would surely come to our aid...although bringing Wolfie into the mix would mean losing the right to remain alpha of my own pack.

Hunter first, my wolf demanded and I opened our mouth into a lupine grin in response to her haste. Unlike me, my animal half wasn't terrified of the consequences of losing our alpha powers. She was simply impatient at the delay in contacting our chosen mate.

On it, I agreed.

But before I could do more than send a lone tendril of thought wisping down the pack bond, I heard the deep rumble of a truck's engine starting up above my head. The hatch enclosing my pit shook in sympathy, explaining why it had been impossible to move the thick wooden boards when I'd strained against the obstruction earlier. No way was I strong enough to push my way out from underneath what sounded like a half-ton pickup truck.

A tarp slapped aside, the door above my head cracked open, and light seeped into my prison cell at last.

Too late. The SSS must have stashed Lia much closer to me than I'd thought, because it hadn't taken Quill long at all to reach my prison. Which meant I was running out of time. Once our captor joined me in the pit, I wouldn't be able to muster sufficient focus to call upon anyone at all.

Save Lia now or save the whole pack later. It wasn't as difficult a choice as I would have thought. Not when losing my own clan only meant I'd no longer be a pack leader, not that my friends would perish upon some crazy outpack male's altar.

Even as those thoughts rushed through my mind, I was frantically shifting into human form and combing through the mud at my feet with fumbling fingers. I needed to call in the cavalry, but I also needed to ensure I could buy enough time for my friends to travel to our remote location.

There! A torn fingernail caught on woven fabric, and I quickly clasped Crew's collar around my throat. Then, knowing I was losing the ability to shift again for several hours due to two transformations in quick succession, I fell back down onto lupine paws and hunched my body into the mud. Rolling my head quickly from side to side, I matted the fur there so completely that the muddy collar became completely invisible around my neck.

Now or never, I told myself, closing my lupine eyes to buy a couple more seconds of focus before the cowboy shifter took me in hand. Rather than trying to grope a final time for my elusive connection to Hunter, I instead contacted the only shifter I was 100% certain I could get through to immediately.

Because I'd been trying to take the easy way out before rather than going for the sure bet. The pack bond I'd been gifted with less than a month earlier was immature and tenuous as it strung a line of connection between me and my young pack mates. But the alpha dominance that backed those links up was sure and strong, a gift solidly granted by my previous pack leader Wolfie Young.

Just as Ginger had been able to sever her tie to me and fling our connection back in my face, I could do the same to Wolfie. But in my case, I wouldn't just be disconnecting one strand of a web...I'd be cutting through the linkage that bound my entire clan together. Basically, I'd be severing my newfound alpha abilities from my body and wrenching my pack mates out of my soul in the process.

Details, details.

Meanwhile, the results would be just as extreme for Wolfie as for me. The mantle's recoil would slap the bloodling alpha in the face with such strength it would surely get his full attention. Then, hopefully, my former pack leader would be annoyed and intrigued enough to follow that blow back to its source. In the process, he'd be able to pull Lia and Savannah out of their prison...assuming he reached us before Quill stopped chasing my tail and turned his attention to the younger halfies.

Of course, I wouldn't be able to lead a clan any longer after breaking the bond. And without the sharp edges of my current alpha abilities to protect those I cared about from the depredations of outpack males, I'd be forced to send my friends and companions home for the sake of their own safety.

But wasn't that the true heart of the matter anyway? If I wasn't a strong enough leader to protect my clan while backed up by the full strength of the alpha mantle, then I didn't deserve the extra powers in the first place.

So even as the falling rain clumped together fur and trickled down through underfluff to my bare lupine skin, I ignored the externals and uncurled my incorporeal human body within the confines of the wolf's skull. There was the thin thread of light connecting me to Wolfie, the line stretched taut by distance and appearing easy to sever. But when I began yanking at the strand with human fingernails, an iron core resisted every effort at dismantlement.

Above my head, distant voices coalesced into words. Then light seeped through clenched lupine eyelids as the hatch above my pit opened yet further. I was running out of time.

Tool use, my wolf whispered. And despite the impending danger and diceyness of the current situation, I had to smile as the animal reminded me what separated humans from wolves.

In case you haven't noticed, we're in fur form at the moment, I bantered back. Good thing incorporeal speech didn't require a mouth because I'd given up on prying apart Wolfie's tether with fingernails and had since moved on to ripping with blunt human teeth. Unfortunately, my jaws were no more effective than my hands had been.

I'm in fur form. You're not, my wolf countered.

Much as it pained me to admit the fact, she was right. I *felt* like I'd been squashed into miniature and stuffed down the wolf's gullet, but my human brain was really just as ethereal as the thread of light I was currently trying to gnaw apart.

Which meant that perhaps I really *could* just imagine a tool and it would appear here in my virtual abode. Perhaps I wasn't forced to rely on clawless human hands to break Wolfie's tether after all.

Even though I'd already closed the wolf's physical eyes, I now clenched shut my virtual human eyes as well. And I begged the heavens for the weapon that fit so perfectly into my human fingers that it felt like it had been made for me—Wolfie's grandfather's sword. After all, since my previous pack leader had given me the katana to symbolize my newfound alpha responsibilities, it seemed like poetic justice that I might use the same device to relinquish said powers.

My imaginary hands were abruptly weighted down by the rough, corded hilt of the katana, and I gasped out a virtual breath of surprise. Wolf intuition aside, I hadn't really thought the gamble would pay off.

But there wasn't time to be amazed at my ability to materialize weapons as I crouched inside my wolf's scheming skull. My captors would be invading my more physical personal space at any moment, and the tether connecting me to Wolfie still pulsed just as strongly as ever.

So, there inside the wolf's skin, I grasped the virtual hilt of Wolfie's grandfather's sword tightly with ten trembling fingers. Then I hacked at the strand of light connecting me to another.

The rebound this time around was so strong that I fell flat on my face, nostrils once again filling with water.

But it was done. I'd called for help.

Now I just needed to delay until my chosen rescuer showed up to save all of our skins.

CHAPTER 25

"Doesn't look like much does she?"

I'd planned to feign weakness, but the truth was that throwing away the alpha mantle had taken a lot more out of me than I'd expected. So there was nothing pretend about my passiveness as one heavy human body after another jumped down to squelch through the muddy pit beside me.

"Looks can be deceiving." This was Quill's voice, his southern drawl no longer sounding so charming now that I understood the depth of his depravity. "So pay close attention."

Then the cowboy shifter's firm tone flickered into laughter as he caught sight of my underwear. I hadn't taken the time to rip the thin layer of cotton off my wolf's body during the minute recently spent in human form, instead choosing to focus on hunting down and then donning Crew's collar during my last seconds alone. Now, as I realized how absurd my bedraggled wolf must look in her Tuesday undies, I regretted the oversight.

"Nice granny panties," the nameless sidekick said, slipping one finger beneath the waistband to pull it taut, then letting the elastic snap back against my fur.

I almost growled, but restrained myself in time. *Sorry to disappoint, boys,* I thought instead. *If I'd known you were going to kidnap me and stuff me in a hole in the ground, I would have sprung for classier lingerie.*

"Let's get her up where we can see her," Quill commanded, the moment of merriment past. My supposed pack mate clearly remembered how I'd taunted him with Lia's stolen lips a few minutes earlier, and even my days-of-the-week panties weren't enough to sidetrack him from his mission.

Two sets of rough hands settled beneath my shoulders and hips, and my wolf twitched despite my efforts to remain completely unmoving. At least I wasn't two-legged while these monsters touched my bare skin. Instead, I felt absurdly grateful for the animal fur that buffered my wolf from our enemies' malicious fingers.

Then my stomach swooped as I was heaved up to land on the edge of the hole. Until this point, I'd kept my eyes squeezed tightly shut, feigning slumber. But with my captors still in the pit below me, I knew my chance to escape had finally arrived.

Rousing my wolf with an effort, I reminded the animal of her marching orders as succinctly as possible. *I'm not going to weigh you down,* I told her. *Because you'll need all the fleetness of foot you can muster. We've got to find cover before we're recaptured.*

She and I both knew that the wolf brain would only be responsible for the first few minutes of our retreat. After that, I'd take back over and buy us more time, keeping the SSS members away from Lia and Savannah for as long as possible. But, for now, our success or failure rested on the head of the wolf.

My animal half didn't answer in words, but I felt her willingness as I carefully disentangled my human mind from her senses and dropped down her throat toward her belly. I didn't want to go so far that I wouldn't be available if she needed me. But I also wasn't willing to repeat my usual mistake of not trusting the animal half to command her own skin, slowing our reaction time in the process. We'd need every bit of skill we could muster to tease the SSS males without being caught.

Then my lupine form was on her feet, running through wet grass that felt heavenly beneath our mud-caked paws. The sensation was distinctly different from my usual experiences of either being in charge or being entirely lost within the darkness of her insides. This time around, I could see our surroundings, albeit at a distance, the sensations similar to watching a movie rather than participating in the action.

As I'd suspected, my prison pit had been located beside a small house surrounded on all sides by trees. An inholding in the national forest, most likely. *Probably no more than an hour's drive from the hotel where our pack holed up*, I mused.

Which meant we were roughly eight hours distant from Wolfie's territory. If I'd had a body, my stomach would have sunk into my shoes. As it was, my human brain drifted a little lower down the wolf's esophagus as I realized I'd made the wrong decision. I should have tried harder to track down local assistance rather than spreading my net so far afield. My new task of keeping Quill and his buddies busy for a third of a sun cycle seemed like an eternity.

"Shit! She's awake!"

Speak of the devil. I didn't look back, but from the sounds behind me I gathered that the second male had emerged from the pit and caught sight of our lupine form streaking away through the rain. Then Quill must have joined his comrade aboveground because energy began gathering in the air between us.

The tingling, hair-raising sensation was similar to the moment just before lightning struck, when electricity accumulated in the earth in preparation for spearing through the unwary. Although not as natural, our current reality was equally dangerous. My ex-captor was preparing to hit my wolf form with an alpha compulsion that her submissive nature had no chance of fighting against.

Based on the evidence of his elongated shift and his supposedly gentle persona, I hadn't thought the cowboy shifter had it in him to order another wolf around. But now I realized that his supposed weakness had only been part of the act, just like his drifter persona and the tale of lost love. All had worked together to lower my defenses and prompt me to accept the cowboy shifter into our clan against both Lia and Hunter's better judgment.

Now, I could finally sense the truth—Quill wasn't a passive, laid-back shifter like Cinnamon. Wolf senses didn't lie, and my animal body's fur was standing on end even as she strained to put more distance between us and the power-hungry male.

We only had one chance of escape left. If I could squash my wolf as I'd done for most of my life, then the upcoming alpha compulsion would roll right off our back just like Hunter's had when the uber-alpha appeared in my life for the first time. Quill's superior dominance wouldn't matter if I had no lupine nature to vanquish.

So I clawed upwards, struggling to dislodge my animal brain before Quill could recapture us with a single word. But it was too late.

"*Halt,*" the cowboy shifter commanded, the directive calm and even as if he knew exactly how his prey would respond.

And he was right. *I guess all those stolen halfie hearts paid off,* I thought as my wolf's muscles froze to the earth.

Once again, we'd been caught effortlessly in Quill's trap.

CHAPTER 26

The pounding rain had picked up even more in the seconds I stood frozen to the earth, so I could barely hear the outpack males advancing. Still, I knew my wolf had only run about fifty feet before our muscles stopped working. Which meant I had roughly thirty seconds to get my act together before we ended up back down in that dark, dirty hole.

"Why are we taking her out now if moon-rise isn't for another six hours anyway?" the nameless partner grumbled as the duo advanced on my frozen form. I felt my stomach rumble as I realized it had to be Saturday afternoon already, meaning I'd lost nearly a day to drugs and claustrophobic dazes. My legs abruptly weakened, and I rolled my eyes at my own psychosomatic reaction.

Wait a minute—I rolled my eyes?

Sure enough, taking stock of my physical sensations proved that my human brain now shared our lupine body with the animal. Which meant I might be able to push the latter aside after all and take to my heels before our captors reached our side.

Here goes nothing.

I strained with all my might against the wolf's usually weak persona. Generally, it took no more than a flick of a virtual finger to toss her back down into the darkness of our shared subconscious. But Quill's compulsion appeared to have locked the wolf in place just as thoroughly as it had pinned our paws to the earth a moment earlier.

But maybe.... Rather than straining against Quill's command, I opted to work sideways this time around. Short of uber-alpha levels of control like Hunter's, a compulsion didn't usually halt involuntary body movements. Otherwise, underlings would all keel over from lack of oxygen to the brain.

So while Quill's barked order made it impossible for me to move my legs or neck, my heart was still pumping and my lungs were still billowing. Plus, I maintained that other involuntary lupine reaction...the urge to scratch.

I tunneled my attention down to an imaginary itch directly beneath Crew's collar. First, I pinpointed it in my mind—just under my left ear, midway down my neck. And as I focused, the creeping sensation slowly became real.

Muddy fur hung up beneath harsh fabric, I thought and felt those wrong-directed hairs tweaking nerve endings in my skin. *Wet, heavy,* I noted, paying attention to the way the collar chaffed against my sensitive flesh. And was that a flea burrowing into the warm cavity underneath?

The imagined itch had become nearly unbearable by the time my wolf reached up with one hind leg to jab at our neckband. But I could have danced and sung inside her body with sheer relief. My ploy had worked!

Now, I'd just have to hope that the SSS's banana extract was oil-based rather than water-based and hadn't been completely washed away by the collar's dunking. And that the wolf's relentless clawing would be sufficient to dislodge whatever trace was left behind.

Scratch, scratch, scratch. The collar moved in a circle around our shared neck, easing the itch and spreading relief through our nerve endings. But I didn't relax because Quill and his partner were still moving ever close behind us. It might already be too late.

Then one lupine nail knocked against the tiny plastic receptacle that some nameless SSS member had sewn into our collar. The claw caught and dug in...and then the faintest aroma of rotten banana filled the air.

Abruptly, my wolf was gone. Or rather, the animal mind had been banished, leaving my human brain in full command of our once-shared lupine body.

Quill was close enough now that I could feel his body heat as one hand reached out to grab me by the ruff. But I was faster. I darted to one side, watching with delight as the cowboy shifter slipped and fell into the muddy ooze beneath our feet.

Then I was racing flat out toward the treeline not far away. Once I reached the forest, I'd have a little breathing room. Time to regroup and get my bearings, time to come up with a more complex plan than my current *escape at all costs.*

"*Stop,* damn you!" Quill roared behind me. I glanced over one shoulder and saw that my enemy had regained his feet and was pulling out what looked like a handgun from a holster beneath his armpit. The SSS member's current compulsion had failed, so he was going for more serious firepower.

Uh oh. Good thing my wolf was still absent and my human brain wasn't required to obey that second command.

I dodged behind a broad pine trunk as the first bullet ricocheted toward me. The next missile clipped the end of my tail as my human reflexes didn't quite manage to dodge in time.

But then I was diving into the midst of a patch of greenbriers, slithering down a ravine, and darting deeper into the forest.

The outpack males' voices dimmed behind me. I'd eluded pursuit.

Now, to see if I could keep Quill and his compatriots from giving up the hunt and turning their attention to the other prisoners for eight long, grueling hours.

**

As soon as I mustered a little breathing room, those dratted Tuesday panties were the first thing to go. I rubbed up against a rough-barked chestnut oak until the underwear slid down off my lupine hips and fell with a damp splat onto the ground at my feet.

Wrinkling my upper lip, I wished I could afford to simply dig a little hole and bury the offending garment right there. But, instead, I picked the fabric up in my mouth and trotted off. I had a plan.

As I'd hoped, my supposed alpha powers turned me into me a prize worth hunting despite the pouring rain. Nearly immediately, in fact, Quill had called in the third SSS member to join him and his partner in their search of the dripping woods, leaving Lia and Savannah alone in the momentary safety of their locked room. In other words, my plan had thus far been successful.

The goal now was to keep all three outpack males so busy searching that they didn't have any leisure in which to molest the girls. To that end, I'd dodged into sight several times, leaving a paw print or purposefully broken twig here and there to signal my progress. It was a difficult game—always staying ahead of my potential captors without letting them lose hope that they'd eventually be able to find me.

But I needed a break. My stomach was rumbling and my brain was getting a little mushy from lack of calories. Plus, despite hours spent comatose within my prison cell, my eyelids were now heavy and begging a dose of REM sleep.

Let me lead, my wolf whispered. Rather than soothing her with platitudes the way I would have in the past, I nodded our shared head. Yes, that was the perfect solution—for my human brain to nap within our shared body while the wolf took command for half an hour or so.

But the wolf didn't boast the same complicated human logic that I found easy to harness. So I wanted to set her up with a good situation before I took a break.

Soon, I promised, speeding up from a walk into a trot. One of my paws was cracked and already becoming infected after being dragged through miles of mud, but I ignored the pain and instead ran forward until I caught sight of a handy snag.

Riiip. The inch-wide shred of pantie that remained behind on the protruding branch stub was just large enough to be noticeable without using up too much of my stash of fabric. And, to my delight, I saw that raindrops were already dragging dirt particles out of the cloth, leaving a whitish color behind.

Perfect. Even Quill's brain-dead sidekick can't miss that, I noted. Then I turned right, wriggling under a deadfall to make the trail more difficult to follow before trotting straight up the nearest hillside.

Another snag, another pantie scrap, another elusive twist in my trail to keep the SSS members scratching their heads while thinking they were edging ever closer to their prey. Then, finally, when the last scrap of underwear was tossed atop a nearby bush, I gave my wolf the reins.

Wake me if you need me, I requested. And, finally, I fell sound asleep.

***

The crunch of breaking bones roused me from what turned out to be a surprisingly effective nap. The sound was obviously not caused by big, worrisome wolf or human bones. Instead, tasty, little rodent bones splintered beneath our sharp lupine teeth.

My animal half had hunted down a snack.

Resourceful wolf, I praised her. But then my human brain rose to look out of our shared eyes, and I had the impulse to take back every word of commendation...plus the hours of slumber that had preceded them. Once again, I'd trusted the wrong partner and let down my pack in the process.

While I'd been sleeping, the rainy day had dimmed into a clear but damp evening. And my wolf had hidden our shared body beneath a rhododendron bush at the edge of a clearing, so I didn't have to worry about being noticed. No, the issue wasn't inability to take in the scene or worry over my own safety...it was the gut-wrenching sight slowly coming into focus before us.

Altars. I remembered one of the barflies mentioning that word on Tuesday evening and wondered now how I hadn't realized that yesterday's farm field was the wrong place entirely for an SSS ritual. Because there had been no sacrificial paraphernalia present there...unlike in our current location, where two huge stones caught the glow of the rising moon on their polished surfaces.

Surfaces that gleamed dark with previous rounds of spilled blood. Surfaces on which two small female figures were even now being bound into place.

Why didn't you wake me earlier? I demanded of the wolf. It was almost too late already. The SSS members must have given up on their hunt and returned to plan A some time ago, figuring two halfies in the hand were better than one in the bush.

I should've been present to dog their footsteps from prison cell to altar.

Maybe there would have been an opportunity to break the girls free. Maybe we could have all escaped already if my animal half hadn't been more interested in rodent snacks than in the safety of our clan.

No chance to free them, my wolf replied simply. Images flashed through our shared mind. Guns, an alert Quill, two other males watching his back. Then, she finished: *You needed rest and food. Now you can save our friends.*

The animal brain wasn't the best at expressing herself, but I could feel her emotions flowing through our shared body. She trusted me to come through with a clever plot to save the day. She figured that after a nap and a field mouse, I'd be capable of springing Lia and Savannah from their sacrificial altars, no sweat.

The wolf had so much faith in me. But I didn't see how I could live up to her expectations. Not when I was naked and defenseless and faced with three armed men.

Speak of the devil. While I'd wavered, Quill decided to get the ball rolling by calling into the half-light: "I know you're out there, Fen. And I'm willing to offer you a deal. Surrender yourself and we'll let these kids go."

He paused, his honey-smooth voice turning ominous as he pulled a knife out of a sheath that hung from his belt. The blade was long and wicked, with a hook at one end perfect for gutting a deer...or a girl.

Savannah moaned in despair, but Lia kept her lips pressed close together as Quill's knife rose seemingly of its own volition to settle in the soft spot at the base of her neck. "So what will it be, Fen?" my once-pack-mate demanded. "Them...or you?"

CHAPTER 27

I had no plan. Just a hope and a promise—a hope that I'd think of something on the fly and a promise to Lia that I wouldn't let the SSS harm another hair on her head. The combination would have to be enough.

Are we able to shift? I asked my wolf. I wasn't sure how much time had passed in wolf body since our last transformation, but I was optimistic that my longer-than-intended nap plus the wolf's snack might have been enough to recharge the relevant muscles. *I guess my wolf was smart to let me rest after all,* I decided.

Rather than remarking upon my change of heart, the animal obediently relaxed her control over our furry body. And I responded by pushing against the inside of her skin, trying to force my way out.

Slowly, ever so slowly, we lost fur and regained thumbs. The transformation was neither fast nor elegant, and I wound up kneeling on the wet leaves of the forest floor rather than standing on two feet. But it had worked.

"*Fen.*" Quill's tone was filled with warning now as he called out a second time into the slowly darkening forest. "I'm losing patience."

I closed my eyes and took a deep breath. It wasn't as if I was dilly-dallying around out here. I was simply trying to ensure that when I walked into the cowboy shifter's trap—because of course his proposed exchange was actually a trap—that I had every possible factor lined up in my favor.

To that end, I spun in a frantic circle, eyes peeled in hopes a weapon might miraculously appear. What I wouldn't give for the sword I'd left behind in the clan vehicle the day before and that I'd used in virtual form only hours earlier. Or for a gun like the one I'd noticed bulging beneath the cowboy shifter's clean, dry shirt when I'd peered out between rhododendron leaves with lupine eyes.

Heck, I'd even take a plastic spoon at this point, I thought, quirking up one side of my mouth as I laughed at my own helplessness. Hunter had been worried I wouldn't be able to go in for the killing blow when the time was right. But neither one of us had envisioned this scenario—me walking up to three enemy shifters naked and entirely unarmed.

Well, not quite entirely unarmed. The pine tree a few paces behind me had cut off all nutrient flow to its lower limbs when the plant grew so tall that new branches shaded out the first attempts. Some of the resulting dead wood was too spindly to do much good. Other possibilities were too high above my head to reach. But one tantalizing branchlet was about two inches thick and looked both tough and sturdy. I suspected the limb would break to create a sharp, jagged point if I grabbed the far end and yanked.

Of course, the sound of breaking wood would also alert my enemies that I was nearby. But I didn't think I currently had the element of surprise on my side anyway. Quill knew me well enough to assume that I wouldn't save my own skin at the expense of my pack.

So I went for it. Edging out from beneath my bush, I leapt up to capture the targeted branch with both hands. And for a moment I dangled a foot above the ground, feet swaying in the air. Just my luck—the limb I'd chosen was stronger than it had initially appeared.

"This is your final warning." I twitched at the sound of Quill's voice, then winced as his sentence was followed by a short shriek of pain. The recipient of the cowboy shifter's wrath had to be Savannah since I knew for a fact Lia would bite through her tongue before she'd emit a sound that she thought would draw me into danger.

Craaaaccck.

I stumbled as I fell, stabbing the sharp end of my new weapon into the tender flesh of my own wrist when stick and arms ended up tangled beneath me in an effort to break my fall. The wound stung and I smiled. This wasn't a sword, but it would do.

I spared only a single moment for one final thought of my absent mate. *Now would be a good time to show up, Hunter,* I called down the invisible and probably absent pack bond. Then I paced forward to meet my destiny.

One of the SSS males had grunted out a surprised query seconds earlier in response to the sound of cracking wood followed by the thud of bare feet falling onto the forest floor. And now I was the one listening to heavy footfalls as they started toward my place of concealment. My wolf pulled my human lips upward into a lupine sneer. Perhaps this would be easier than I'd thought after all.

Just a little closer, I begged the outpack male. If a single SSS member set foot within the seclusion of the forest all on his lonesome, I'd soon have two enemies rather than three to deal with. Between the element of surprise, my pointy stick, and the anger that kept my animal half rampant behind my eyes, I didn't doubt for a moment that I'd be able to make short work of any shifter one-on-one.

But Quill was too smart to allow his party to be split up. "*No*," he commanded, wasting an alpha compulsion on a compatriot who I suspected would have obeyed a human command just as easily. "Fen will come out on her own. And *quickly* if she doesn't want me to start carving fingers and toes off little girls."

His words seemed to turn the air ten degrees colder in an instant and I shivered. The cowboy shifter wasn't bluffing—instead, I heard gleeful anticipation in his voice.

So I held the branch as loosely as I could, hoping it would look like a walking stick rather than a weapon.

Then I stepped out from amid my leafy cover.

***

While I'd been harvesting a half-assed weapon, the sun had fully set. But the rising moon was already bright enough that I could easily make out the expression on Quill's face as I emerged from my woodland lair.

He was gloating. His eyes danced with the knowledge that he'd soon capture a halfie pack leader without having to relinquish either young girl from his clutches. And while I'd like to say that pride goeth before a fall...even though I was armed with a pointy stick, the odds were still definitively stacked in the SSS's favor.

Not that I planned to let my enemy realize I felt that way. "I'm here," I said firmly, pacing forward slowly in order to give myself time to think. Bluffing came as naturally as breathing, so I continued to keep my shoulders high and my chin raised as I emulated an unbeatable alpha. The playacting probably wouldn't do any good, but it also couldn't hurt. "Release the girls and you can do whatever you want with me," I finished.

Unfortunately, my adversary wasn't so easily swayed. Ignoring my posturing, he ground out a truncated order. "Drop the..."

But rather than finishing the sentence, Quill paused and took a closer look at the weapon I held loosely in one hand. "Well, I was going to say *sword*," he finished, laughter now evident in his voice. "But it appears that you've come to a gunfight with a stick." Then his voice hardened. "Still, you can put it down. *Now.*"

The knife that had drifted groundward as his attention focused on me now rose once more to settle against the smooth skin of Lia's neck. One erratic movement and our aggressor could easily slice through the halfie's jugular, ending her life before I could so much as scream in disbelief.

He needs to harvest Lia's heart while it's still beating, I reminded myself. But, despite my best efforts at mustering confidence, my fingers loosened involuntarily from around my hard-earned branch. I couldn't risk a pack mate's life based only on my judgment of Quill's character...or lack thereof.

Still, I gave the weapon a little forward momentum as it fell so the stick landed only a few feet away from my enemies' feet. If I was able to edge just a little closer, then the branch would be there waiting for me to snatch it back up....

Although that first hope was a little far-fetched, my unruly toss had another unintended consequence. Quill lowered his guard in response to what must have appeared a feeble attempt to strike out at him. "Not even close, girl," he taunted with a short laugh. "Now hold your hands out to your sides and walk over here slowly so Mick can bind them."

The now-named shifter was the same outpack male who had snapped my granny panties, and he was even more interested in my unclad human form than he had been in lupine lingerie. Mick's eyes burned into the bare skin of my breasts and crotch, and I had to force myself not to shield my exposed flesh with arms and hands. Or perhaps to lunge forward and smack the guy across his greedy face. Still, the time wasn't yet ripe for me to strike, so I simply paced obediently toward my future captor.

Except Mick might not earn that label after all. Because I noticed Lia and Savannah sharing a quick glance behind our enemies' backs, proving that I'd underestimated both girls. Far from the cowed captives they'd at first appeared, they seemed to have cooked up some sort of plan between them.

Savannah, especially, had initially appeared so beaten down that I'd assumed she'd lie back and accept her fate. But that persona had only been an act. Now that the enemies' eyes were all trained on me, the bound halfie struggled erect. Then, doing her best to keep herself out of her captors' line of sight, she wriggled toward the edge of her altar stone.

Unfortunately, I had a feeling Quill was too alert to be taken by surprise. *Time for a little evasive action.*

"I've been wracking my brain all afternoon," I lied loudly, halting all forward momentum as I snared the enemy males' attention more fully once again. "The name Faye sounded so familiar to me, and I couldn't quite figure out why. Then I realized. Wasn't she that bitch who was caught sleeping around a few All-Packs ago?"

Quill jolted backwards as if he'd been physically struck. Whether the B word or the implications of my lie had done the trick was irrelevant. Regardless, the cowboy shifter was thoroughly knocked off his game by my on-the-fly fairy tale. "She would never..." he spluttered.

I knew my adversary would figure out pretty quickly that I'd neither seen nor heard of Faye before he spoke her name in that VW bus. After all, I couldn't so much as weave her last name or her hair color into my story— I'd honestly never known the woman existed before Quill dropped his star-crossed history on me.

The question was—would the cowboy shifter see through my bluff before the girls' plan bore fruit?

Ah, here we go. A pencil was fumbled out of a waistband...just not by the girl I'd assumed would possess the small weapon. Instead, Savannah was the one who shrieked out an attack cry, Savannah was the one who lunged forward, and Savannah was the one who fell into the unnamed captor's outstretched arms.

"What the..." he began. The outpack male had reached for the girl, I realized, out of some nearly forgotten sense of chivalry rather than in an effort to recapture a prisoner who was already restrained hand and foot. But when those bound hands raised and stabbed a pointy graphite tip into the male's open eye, his scream was gut-wrenching.

The SSS member fell to the ground, writhing as he cradled his injured face with both arms. And without free hands and legs to halt her descent, Savannah plummeted earthward right along with him. But the spunky halfie shuffled to one side as soon as she landed, bracing her back against the altar even as Lia completed her shift atop the other standing stone.

My youngest pack mate must have begun calling on her wolf the moment I stepped into the clearing in order to have so quickly gained fur. And, even so, her transformation was far from smooth. She was excited and scared, I knew, Quill's knife only inches away from her jugular and who knows what fate on the horizon if she failed. But with her captor's attention trained on me and then on his injured compatriot, the teenager was able to not only don fur but also to wriggle her way out of the now-loose ropes that had previously bound her wrists and ankles together.

And then the fight was on. It still wasn't a fair fight—a tired halfie wolf, a tied teenager wielding a pencil, and me with the pointy stick I'd just now scooped back up off the ground against two armed and able-bodied men. But as Lia leapt from one stone to the other and ended up crouched against her new friend's back, I knew we made up in grit what we lacked in firepower. For the first time all day, I truly believed all three of us would make it out of there alive.

But I didn't have time to join my companions beside the standing stone because Quill had finally gotten his act together and was reaching for his handgun. Mick was a bit slower on the draw, but I could tell from the look in the lead SSS member's eyes that my almost-pack-mate wasn't going to bluff this time around. He'd aim for my shoulder or leg—not quite close enough to the head or chest to kill me outright but still causing a serious enough wound that I'd be forced to stay put while he ripped out my beating heart.

Not happening, my wolf growled. We didn't have time to think or to plan, just to lunge at the greatest threat in exactly the way Hunter had trained us to.

It wasn't a killing blow, but it wasn't meant to be a killing blow. Our goal was simply to get rid of the gun so our fight wouldn't end before it really began.

And we succeeded. I heard the bullet burst through the barrel and explode out into the air at the same moment I felt the pain in my forearm. But it didn't matter. My sword—my stick—whatever—had met its mark.

As I watched, the smoking hunk of metal skittered away across abruptly invisible leaves. A well-timed cloud had crossed in front of the moon, and Quill roared his rage as the weapon he depended upon to maintain his competitive edge disappeared into momentary darkness.

Then, far closer than I'd dared to hope, I heard an answering cry rend the night. One wolf howled, then two, then an entire pack.

My clan had finally come to our aid.

CHAPTER 28

They entered the clearing from every side. Hunter's huge brindled wolf was flanked by two ginger-haired canines and one gray—my entire pack united at last. From the other direction, Wolfie and his mate soared forward ahead of an even larger number of furry marauders, their feet moving so quickly that pads barely touched the ground.

Without conscious thought, I reached out with the pack sense to greet them. But the only tether I found was the one linking me to Hunter. Every other thread of the tangled cat's cradle that had recently bound our small clan together had since disintegrated into the warm summer night.

Still, the glowing strand linking me to my mate remained, and I couldn't resist brushing the lightest finger across our tantalizing connection. In response, my mate immediately turned his head to meet my gaze with eyes that glowed pale gold in the returning moonlight.

Thank you for coming, I told him, not sure he'd hear the words but knowing my mate would at least see the welcome in my eyes.

Thank you for calling me, he answered, his reply clear and warm within my mind.

The simple sentence was a soothing balm plastering over the aching hole in my gut, and my hunched shoulders settled down from around my ears for the first time since I'd cast Hunter out of our shared hotel room thirty-six hours earlier. My relief was almost tangible.

But there wasn't time for further honeyed words because Quill didn't give up easily. I smelled bananas—a preemptive strike against Hunter's uber-alpha abilities—and then the air around me was abruptly consumed by dense black smoke.

Coughing, I stumbled with watering eyes toward where I thought Lia and Savannah might have been located. It was impossible to see the girls through the haze, but I was able to use my bond with Hunter as a guideline to orient me in the abrupt pitch darkness. *Just a few more steps this way....*

Then hairs abruptly stood erect on my arms as Quill transformed far too close to my exhausted human body. His wolf was invisible amidst the fumes, but I could tell my enemy was present as easily as I could tell that Hunter was still racing toward me. The former's hunger and anger were a palpable presence now, and I knew without being told that Quill had one intention and one intention alone—to eat at least one halfie heart before he fled the field of battle this night.

No! I screamed within my own mind. I couldn't—wouldn't—let my opponent leap atop the girls we'd all converged upon this clearing to protect.

So, despite the fact that my adversary now boasted sharp teeth and claws to back up his claims, I stepped boldly in front of him. "You'll have to go through me first," I whispered harshly. I couldn't muster any impressive volume due to a smoke-tightened throat, but I was pretty sure grimness would get the message across.

My enemy didn't appear at all chastened though. Instead, he continued to stalk closer until I could see his wolf easily through the man-made fog. The huge dark shape was so near, in fact, that I could have reached out and patted his tremendous head.

Not that I wanted to. Not when Quill appeared to be elated at the opportunity to snare me instead of the weaker teenagers.

I could feel the SSS member's hot breath on my bare shin when he halted, opening his mouth into a lupine snarl wrought with anticipation. Hard animal eyes bored into mine and I found myself unable to move. My chest tightened and my vision tunneled, even my heart slowing its beat in the face of Quill's silent compulsion.

So this is what death looks like.

And then a huge brindled wolf was flying through the air toward my opponent. Hunter didn't bother with a warning blow, simply landed atop the other beast's back and crunched down with iron jaws. Immediately, Quill shuddered, legs losing their ability to hold him upright as his spine snapped. Life fled his dark eyes in an instant.

Rather than letting his deceased prey go, though, Hunter instead fell to the ground with his enemy's ruff still firmly clamped between his teeth. Then the uber-alpha shook his head so vigorously that blood splattered through the air and landed on my cheek.

I didn't look away as my mate tore into the shifter who had killed innocent women and who had tried to do the same to me and my friends. For long moments, the uber-alpha growled and ripped and battered, not stopping until Quill had become an unrecognizable lump of meat and fur splayed across the wet ground.

My mate was a beast. He was wild and rough and barbaric.

And utterly glorious.

I could hardly take my eyes away from Hunter's welcome form long enough to peer out through the thinning fog. But I had to check on the rest of my pack, and especially on the teenage girls who had so recently been lying atop twin sacrificial altars in preparation for losing their hearts.

Because there was still that final uninjured SSS male to deal with. Savannah had taken down one captor with a pencil to the eye, Hunter had made short work of the other, but Mick was still unaccounted for.

I hoped that with so many shifters rushing to our aid, Lia and Savannah would have been safe from the final shifter's aggression. But I wouldn't believe it until I saw the girls with my own eyes. So I wrenched my gaze away from Hunter's depredations with an effort and scanned the clearing.

The first form I was able to pick out through the clearing smoke was Ginger, the trouble twin resembling nothing so much as an avenging goddess as she stood two-legged and naked beneath the moon. Her brother was still in fur form at her feet, while Glen surged upward into humanity even as he caught my eye. In response to my questioning gaze, my steadfast beta stepped aside as soon as his transformation was complete, allowing me to take in the huddle of female limbs on the ground behind him.

I caught my breath. *No!* We'd been too late. *I'd* been too late.

But then Lia moved, the knife in her right hand slicing through the final rope binding her friend in place. And the two girls rose arm in arm, stiff and a little wary but also clearly giddy with relief. They bounced and hugged with the resilience of youth, wide smiles opening their faces as they realized they were encircled by friends instead of enemies at last.

Just as I was now being encircled by Hunter's strong arms. He was flecked with guts and goo, but I didn't care. I squeezed him so hard I thought I might break a rib, and he hugged me back with equal vigor.

For the first time in days, my muscles relaxed and my wolf released her wary stance. We'd succeeded. We'd survived.

And with Hunter in my arms, I was finally home.

EPILOGUE

I slept fitfully even though I had little reason to complain. My bullet hole—a flesh wound only—had long since been cleaned, and members of both my pack and Wolfie's were now spread out across soft beds in the adjoining hotel rooms. We were all safe and alive and together.

Well, not quite together. Hours earlier, pack mate after pack mate had invited me to join them in a post-battle jumble of furry limbs. But it hadn't felt right to bed down with other shifters when the network of incandescent filaments that bound us together as a cohesive whole had been severed by my own free will.

So I thanked each friend but declined their advances. And, one by one, my companions had acceded to my wishes and left me alone.

But now, isolated in my solitary den, I dreamed of a deep, dark hole in the ground. I dreamed of Quill ripping the still-beating heart out of Lia's chest. And I dreamed of the agony in Hunter's eyes when I'd cast my mate out of the pack two mornings prior.

Only when a warm, furry body leapt up onto the bed beside me did I finally jolt out of my fitful drowsing. There was no need to open my eyes as the heavy weight settled into the hollow between knees and stomach. Instead, I simply smelled sassafras with a hint of agitated spring water and knew I was safe.

The thread of sound that I realized was my own whimpering eased as Hunter shifted into human form just long enough to pull me up against his long, lean body. "Shhh," he whispered, stroking my hair. "I'm here."

I meant to open my eyes and respond. But, instead, my mate's soft puffs of breath tickling against the inside of my ear lulled me into a slumber as deep as the one I'd enjoyed when my wolf took the lead during our game of hide and seek a few hours earlier. With Hunter at my side, I could finally let go.

But my mate was gone when I woke again, this time to late morning sunlight streaming through my window. Instead of the uber-alpha, a red-haired bombshell perched on the edge of my bed.

Ginger was fully clad this morning and just as perfectly coiffed as ever. Looking at her now, in fact, I was pretty sure the trouble twin hadn't so much as chipped a fingernail while single-handedly tearing Mick to shreds the night before. She'd looked like a raging beast when I first reached her side, her worry over Lia's safety completely squashing her usual civilized facade of humanity. But the essence of sure-of-herself pack princess had since returned with a vengeance.

I breathed a sigh of relief that lasted...oh, about as long as it took for my companion to open her mouth. "Wolfie says the pack bond might regrow," Ginger told me without preamble, raising one eyebrow as she waited impatiently for my response.

I was barely awake. My mouth tasted like old socks, and my throat was as dry as a desert ravine. But, okay, it looked like we were really going to get into this here and now. "What are you trying to say, Ginger?" I croaked out.

"I'm *saying*," she began, deleting the mitigating word that held no place on her tart tongue, "that we can still be a pack. I know you want to ditch us, to tell us to move back in with our old clan. But that's not happening. Once you're all healed up and ready to go, we're coming right along with you."

"Coming with me where?" I asked gently. "Coming with me to wander through outpack territory hoping we won't get snatched up by another sociopath who thinks halfies make good appetizers to prepare the palate for a pack-princess lunch? Coming with me to watch your cousin traumatized all over again?"

I knew I'd struck a nerve when Ginger glanced aside, and I smiled grimly at my success. I wanted our clan to remain united as much as anyone. But it was time for us both to face reality. Whether or not I'd been a capable alpha in the past, I no longer boasted the strength necessary to lead us to safety.

So, risking getting slapped, I reached out with my right hand and slid workmanlike digits between the trouble twin's slender fingers. "I appreciate your loyalty," I told her. "But without the alpha mantle, it's just not safe for me to drag Lia around hither and yon any longer."

My unoccupied left hand tightened unconsciously around the envelope that Wolfie had dropped off in my room the night before. Truth be told, I wasn't actually going to be wandering aimlessly once my bullet wound healed. But Ginger didn't need to know that right away.

Not when my goal was for her to accept responsibility for her own safety and for that of our shared friends. To let our pack drift apart as organically as the threads that once bound us together had disintegrated into the summer air the afternoon before.

"Then ask Hunter to let you move back into Haven," Ginger demanded, ice-blue eyes flashing. She wasn't willing to let the issue drop and my throat tightened as I realized the trouble twin really *did* care about me as a friend, not just as a crush. Otherwise, she wouldn't have brought up my mate's ability to reverse the decree that had kicked me out of Wolfie's pack in the first place. No, her words now were as much of a show of acceptance as I'd ever get for letting the uber-alpha into my life and my heart.

Still, Ginger's suggestion—while the easy way out—wasn't the right solution. "I could," I agreed. "But I won't."

"You won't?" Ginger leapt to her feet, unable to sit still any longer now that anger filled her body with unharnessed potential. She paced from bed to door and back again. "You won't ask him for one little favor to make your life better? He'd give it to you in heartbeat."

"I would."

The deep male voice carried easily through the closed door and I smiled. Ginger had clearly begged my mate for a minute alone with me. But while Hunter had been willing to step away from my bedside, the uber-alpha hadn't gone far.

I was glad.

So I spoke to them both when I answered. "I know he would," I said. "But back when Hunter kicked me out of Haven in the first place, he realized I needed that nudge if I was ever going to flee my safe but constraining little nest. He said I'd thank him for it later, and he was right. This is me thanking you, Hunter, for helping me learn who I really am. Or at least for prodding me into taking the first step in that direction."

Then I turned my attention back to the girl who had sunken down onto the bed beside me once more. The girl who had been a true friend, even if a little scattershot with her emotions. "But *you* don't need to remain a part of Wolfie's pack forever," I told her. "If anyone in our little clan had the potential to grow into an alpha's abilities, it was you. So rest and regroup...and then spread your wings and fly."

It was true. Ginger had led our fur-form hunts for a reason—she possessed the strength of will necessary to turn a group of independent-minded werewolves into a cohesive pack. Once she matured a little and learned to mind her tongue and passions, the teenager would become a powerful alpha. I was proud to think I'd had a small hand in her growth...even if it meant losing a friend and pack mate in the process.

I think we were both crying a little when Ginger hugged me one last time. "Okay," she muttered. Then, eyes flashing, she landed one last peck on my lips before flouncing out the door and into her future. My mate growled at the twin's forwardness but otherwise held his peace.

Watching her go, I knew that Ginger would be fine. She'd have Cinnamon at her back, and Lia would remain her full-time project until the younger girl overcame any post-traumatic stress developed as a result of her imprisonment. Maybe they'd even form a clan of their own some day.

Still, the hole in my gut felt cavernous as my mate slipped in through the entranceway that the trouble twin had left gaping wide open. "What will you do next?" he asked, pushing the door closed behind him.

I swallowed down my sorrow, then flourished the envelope I'd hidden beneath the covers to keep it away from Ginger's keen nose and eyes. "Wolfie brought me a note from my mom last night," I told him. "From the parent I haven't seen in twelve years. The human who couldn't stand the thought of living among werewolves and who was willing to orphan her daughter if that's what it took to get out from under the beasts' terrifying thumbs."

The uber-alpha's nostrils flared as I spoke and his hands closed into fists. One of these days, I was going to have to learn what it was about halfies and their human parents that pushed his buttons.

But my mate quickly squelched his own emotions, sinking down into the spot that was still warm and indented in the shape of Ginger's well-padded bum. "Go on," he said, his fingers trailing up my arm as if he couldn't quite manage to keep his hands off me when we were in such close proximity.

I didn't mind. I felt the same way.

Still, I needed that appendage free in order to pull the invitation out of its envelope. So I shifted over to lean against my mate's broad chest instead, managing not to sever our connection even as I extricated my arm from his light caress.

Despite now possessing two working hands, I nearly couldn't pull the small black card out of its sheath because my fingers were shaking so violently. The paper boasted silver lettering and ornamentation that shone against the dark background like a wedding invitation turned on its head. There was my mother's name and my father's, a date, a time, a place.

A little line drawing of a gravestone.

"I've been invited to my father's funeral," I told Hunter. "And I think I really have to go."

FROM THE AUTHOR

Did you enjoy Fen's adventure? If so, I hope you'll consider writing a review. Your kind words keep me writing and help others decide whether to take a chance on a new author.

Stay tuned—Fen's story will continue in Packless, *due out in summer 2016. And while you wait, why not dive into my complete Wolf Rampant trilogy? You can download a FREE e-copy of book one and of the spinoff serial if you sign up for my email list at www.aimeeeasterling.com.*

Thank you so much for reading. You are why I write.

Made in the USA
Lexington, KY
30 June 2016